S

Samantha Alexander lives in Lincolnshire with
a variety of animals including her thoroughbred horse, Bunny, and a pet goose called
Bertie. Her schedule is almost as busy and
exciting as her plots – she writes a number of
columns for newspapers and magazines, is a
teenage agony aunt for BBC Radio Leeds and
in her spare time she regularly competes in
dressage and showjumping.

Books by Samantha Alexander
available from Macmillan

HOLLYWELL STABLES

1. *Flying Start*
2. *The Gamble*
3. *The Chase*
4. *Fame*
5. *The Mission*
6. *Trapped*
7. *Running Wild*
8. *Secrets*

RIDERS

1. *Will to Win*
2. *Team Spirit*
3. *Peak Performance*
4. *Rising Star*
5. *In the Frame*
6. *Against the Clock*
7. *Perfect Timing*
8. *Winning Streak*

HOLLYWELL STABLES

8

Secrets

SAMANTHA ALEXANDER

**MACMILLAN
CHILDREN'S BOOKS**

*Samantha Alexander and Macmillan Children's Books
would like to thank the riding department at Lillywhites
for lending us clothes featured on the covers.*

*We would also like to thank all at Suzanne's Riding School,
especially Suzanne Marczak, Jo and Vero.*

First published 1995 by Macmillan Children's Books

Reprinted 1999 by Macmillan Children's Books
a division of Macmillan Publishers Limited
25 Eccleston Place, London SW1W 9NF
and Basingstoke

Associated companies throughout the world

ISBN 0 330 34202 9

3 5 7 9 8 6 4

A CIP catalogue record for this book is available from the British Library

Typeset by CentraCet, Cambridge
Printed and bound in Great Britain by Mackays of Chatham plc, Kent

Chapter One

"It's a death trap, Mel. There's no way I'm jumping it!"

We were standing in the main arena of the local county show looking at a new show-jump which anyone could see was downright dangerous.

It was a wooden bridge called a ha-ha with a stile at the end and Blake said it was there to draw in the crowds, to create a spectacle. There had already been an article in the local paper comparing it to a bank which had been used at Olympia, where a horse had been killed.

"I'm pulling out, I don't care about the prize money." Blake screwed up his entry number with contempt. "Somebody's got to make a stand!"

"Mel, Blake!" Sarah, my stepmother, came charging across the arena waving a catalogue at us, her red hair flying back, making her look more like a film star than a romantic novelist.

"Of all the pigheaded old fossils," she fumed. "They won't change their minds, they won't budge an inch!"

1

We'd left her wrangling with the stewards while we went to have a second look at the ha-ha. I couldn't believe any course designer would expect a horse to canter over such a flimsy bridge and then somehow jump the four-foot stile at the end. It was ridiculous.

"They say it cost a fortune to build and it's perfectly safe." Sarah was beside herself with frustration. "They won't take a blind bit of notice."

The loudspeaker crackled into life. "Would all competitors now leave the arena as the grade A championship is about to commence."

"Not if I can help it." Sarah whipped round and marched out of the arena.

I knew exactly how she felt, I was boiling up with fury too. "Blake, you've got to do something!"

Back in the collecting ring, grooms and competitors were milling round, apprehensive and trying to make a decision. Blake marched up to Daniel Lamond, one of the top young riders, who was leaning against the rails signing autographs, his groom already warming up his horse.

"Forget it, Kildaire, there's no way I'm pulling out. There's too much money at stake."

Sarah came out of the stewards' office shaking her head.

My brother, Ross, pushed through the crowds leading Colorado, a beautiful skewbald who was only 14.2 hands but rated as one of the best jumpers in the country. He and Blake had already taken the show by storm, winning a speed class with a scorching round which left the others standing. If he'd gone into the championship he'd have probably won best horse in show.

"I'm not jumping," said Blake, as he led Colorado back to the temporary stables.

"Mel! Mel!" A purple mohican hairstyle burst through a crowd of onlookers and Trevor, our full-time groom, appeared at my side, hot and gasping. "It's chaos on the stall." He tried to get his breath. "They're all going dotty over the fan club – I can't cope. Where've you been?"

I suddenly remembered that I was supposed to relieve him half an hour ago, but I'd got totally taken up with the show-jumping.

We'd had the Hollywell Stables, Sanctuary for Horses and Ponies, stand on the showground for the full two days. We'd completely sold out of Hollywell T-shirts, baseball caps and mugs and it looked as if we desperately needed more membership forms. Poor Trevor – he'd been left by himself all morning.

"But what about the show-jumping?" I said, but he was already dragging me by the arm through the throngs of people back to our stand, which luckily wasn't too far from the main arena.

"Excuse me dear, how much is this?" A woman

in a multicoloured hat thrust a Hollywell tea towel under my nose. There was a queue of people clutching merchandise and I could immediately see what Trevor meant. My little sister Katie and her friend Danny were supposed to be helping but Trevor said they'd sloped off to the goat tent hours ago and he hadn't seen them since.

"The first rider in the ring, ladies and gentlemen, is number 28, Daniel Lamond, with the very experienced Earl Grey."

My hand froze in mid-air as I handed a woman her change. I could hear the hoofbeats on the hard ground, and the crowd fell silent as he went through the treble combination. It would be the bridge next.

"Mel, come back!"

I pushed my way through the ten-deep crowd and felt the sweat starting to run down my back from the heat. I nearly fell over a man sitting on a shooting stick and then ducked behind a television camera.

The huge grey was lumbering down to the bridge with his ears pricked forward. Daniel held him between hand and leg keeping up the impulsion and leapt on to the bridge off a perfect stride.

One-two-three. Check, check. Earl Grey bunched his hindquarters underneath him and popped out over the stile, making it look easy. A

4

huge whoop went up from the crowd and the commentator complimented Daniel's superb riding. A clear round.

"Blake, what's going on?"

Blake, Ross and Sarah were standing at the entrance to the collecting ring with their eyes glued on the next horse in the ring, a heavy dun cob who didn't appear to have any brakes.

"He'll never hold him over the bridge," said Blake, raking his hand through his dark hair, as edgy as a cat on hot bricks.

Daniel Lamond swaggered across the collecting ring looking smug. A reporter from the local radio station stuck a microphone in front of him and he said, "It's no problem at all. It just separates the men from the boys." He swung a quick glance in Blake's direction.

"The jumped-up little nerd," said Sarah; and I couldn't believe I had once thought Daniel Lamond was the biggest hunk in Britain.

"And that's another clear round," said the commentator, sounding almost disappointed that there hadn't been any spills or thrills. The crowd clapped mechanically and started drifting towards the shire-horse parade in the next ring.

The big dun horse ploughed back into the collecting ring, streaming with sweat. Maybe the bridge wasn't so bad after all. Maybe we'd over-reacted?

"I don't believe it," said Blake, staring at a pretty chestnut mare warming up over a cross pole.

"What is it? What's the matter?" Ross whipped off his extra-dark sunglasses and followed Blake's gaze.

"It's impossible," said Blake. "It can't be."

A man wearing a cowboy hat scuffed across the deep sand and put the jump up by at least a foot. "Now hold her together," he barked out at the inexperienced looking girl on top. "Come on Goldie, you can do it!"

Goldie was the chestnut mare. Blake told us that her show name was Gold Crest Lady, and that she was an old hand on the show-jumping circuit. She'd been around for ever and had never refused in her life. Next to Colorado she was the bravest horse he'd ever known.

"But that's just it," he growled. "I saw her only last week at the Royal. She was so lame she could barely walk. How could she have recovered this quickly?"

"How dare you tell me what to do? It's none of your business!" The man with the cowboy hat glared at Blake as if he was completely mad and grabbed hold of Goldie's reins. "Haven't you lot caused enough trouble already?"

Goldie jerked her head back in alarm, her soft

6

brown eyes filling up with panic. It was impossible to see if her legs were swollen because she was wearing protective boots.

"But I saw this horse only last week." Blake tried again. "She can't possibly be sound enough—"

"Are you going in or not?" An official stepped forward, anxious to get the next horse into the ring.

"Dad, I don't think I want to . . ." The girl on Goldie's back looked a nervous wreck and was frantically entwining her fingers in Goldie's mane.

"Go on, off you go, I've not spent all this money for nothing." The man yanked Goldie forward and they entered the main ring.

The crowd fell silent and the bell clamoured into life. Any minute now and the girl would have to start her round. Goldie moved obediently forward and cantered towards the first fence.

"What's happening?" Trevor appeared at my side, clutching the cash box. "I couldn't stand it any longer," he gasped. "I can't see anything back there!"

Sarah held up her hand, shielding her eyes from the sun.

Goldie turned towards the double gates, her ears cocked forward, her stride lengthening. The girl on her back was completely hopeless; she couldn't ride for toffee.

7

"Goldie's carrying her round," Blake breathed. "She's totally outclassed."

"So how's she going to tackle the bridge?"

We all held our breath as Goldie launched herself over the wall off a wrong stride.

"Good girl," Blake murmured under his breath. "She's doing it all by herself."

The girl bounced up and down, becoming more unbalanced with every jump. This is what I hated to see; parents so keen to do well that they spent a fortune on expensive horses just so their children could enter the big classes. It was an attempt to buy success and it was pointless. This girl would have more fun on a riding school horse doing the minimus.

"She's on the wrong leg." Ross's voice was as taut as a tightrope as Goldie fought to keep her balance round a tight corner. There was no sign of any lameness. Her bold stride was eating up the ground.

Through the treble combination. Perfect timing. Goldie was trying her heart out. Now the bridge. Steady. Steady her. She was going too fast. Goldie's head came up – a moment's hesitation.

The girl immediately started flapping her arms and legs. It was the worst thing she could have done. Goldie lunged forward. She was going much too fast, totally unbalanced, her legs were all over the place.

The whole audience gasped in horror as Goldie plunged on to the narrow bridge and her entire hindquarters slipped underneath her. It was horrible to see. She was sliding all over, scrabbling to stay upright. It was like a skating rink.

"Oh no!" Sarah's hand flew up to her mouth.

"She's going to fall!" Trevor yelled out.

Goldie hit the ground with a sickening thud. Thankfully the girl was thrown forward, clear of the flailing hoofs, both her feet coming out of the stirrups.

"I told you something like this would happen," Sarah screamed at one of the officials.

"She can't get up!" Blake shouted. Ross was already ducking under the ropes, Trevor right behind him. "She's hurt." Blake was glaring at the man in the cowboy hat. "Goldie's hurt!"

Chapter Two

"She's broken her leg." A new vet in the area called Tom Drummond stood in the arena and gave his verdict.

"But it doesn't have to mean the end!" Sarah gave Mr Drummond an eyeball-to-eyeball glare. To our horror he'd already advised Goldie's owners to have her put down on the spot.

"She deserves a chance." Blake held on to Goldie's reins, rubbing her ears, trying to get her to relax. Her injured foreleg was held up at an awkward angle, the sweat was running off her in streams. "It's all right darling, everything's going to be OK."

The girl had been taken off to the first aid tent immediately although there was nothing wrong with her apart from shock, but she was so hysterical she wouldn't have been much use to Goldie anyway. Her dad was more interested in examining the expensive show-jumping saddle which had been slung on the ground than looking at Goldie's leg.

Three stewards in identical bowler hats talked

into walkie-talkies and within minutes the horse ambulance came trundling across the arena, a white trailer with a blue cross on the side and, according to Sarah, specially padded inside just like our Hollywell horsebox.

"Get the screens across," one of the stewards yelled, looking scathingly at the gathering crowds. "Next they'll be taking photographs."

"It's all right Goldie, we'll soon get you out of here." The poor mare was shaking convulsively and her breathing sounded terrible.

It was a nightmare. Her near foreleg was just dangling in the air, the fetlock and hoof waving limply like something out of a horror movie. If I looked at it too much I knew I'd be sick, so I concentrated on stroking her nose and trying to ease the fear and the pain.

More men appeared, struggling with green canvas sheeting and propping up poles. Suddenly the whole showground was blotted out and all we could see was the inside of the horse ambulance and the ropes and pulleys ready to winch her in.

The message went out on the loudspeaker for a second time. "Would all acting veterinary surgeons please make their way to the main arena. Thank you."

It was a standard procedure to seek a second opinion and there were three vets on duty that day. James happened to be one of them. He also

11

happened to be Sarah's fiancé and our local vet. And there was no way he'd let Goldie die.

"Where is he?" Sarah hissed, wracked with nerves and well aware that all the stewards were in agreement with Drummond that Goldie should be put down.

Ross had last seen him attending to a prize-winning bull who'd cut his leg open on a car bumper, and that was right over the other side of the showground.

"Come on James, come on."

The tension in the closed-off area was becoming unbearable. The girl's dad had turned white and didn't seem to know how to handle the situation. Tom Drummond looked thunderous and it was obvious the stewards just wanted the whole problem to go away. Goldie hopped on three legs and then stood gasping, her pretty, delicate face contorted in agony. Surely the injection she'd had should start numbing the pain soon? The smell of churned-up grass, fear, sweat and blood made me feel nauseous. How much longer?

"Poor old lady," said Blake, mopping at the sweat which was running into her eyes. "She doesn't deserve this."

"Broken legs can be mended," Trevor blurted out. "What about that dressage horse, Rembrandt, or whatever his name was?"

Mr Drummond looked at him as if he was

something the cat had dragged in. "When I want your opinion I'll ask for it."

"You might be a vet," Trevor flew back at him, "but we're from Hollywell Stables – we believe where there's life there's hope."

"Sentimental money-wasting trouble-makers if you ask me." Mr Drummond turned round muttering under his breath just as Sarah was about to fly to our defence.

"It's James!" I'd never been more pleased to see the familiar tousled brown head poke round the canvas.

"Now then old girl, let's take a look at you, shall we?"

Goldie stood as still as she could while James examined her leg, but no matter how gentle he tried to be it was impossible not to cause her pain.

"It's a clean fracture of the cannon bone, it's not come through the skin. I believe it can be plated."

James stood up to his full height and faced Tom Drummond. "If we can get her to Newmarket in the next few hours I believe we can save her life." James had never sounded more determined.

"Yes!" Trevor clenched his fist. I could feel my cheeks creasing into a grin.

"We've got to strap it immediately. There's no time to lose."

"I disagree." Tom Drummond stood with his

13

arms folded and his feet apart in defiance. "Number one. Even if the operation is a success, which is a long shot, she'll never be able to show-jump again. Number two. She's an old mare; she's no good for breeding or anything else for that matter. And number three, the owner informs me she's not insured for medical bills, so I pose the question: just who is going to pay for it?"

The cowboy hat nearly fell to the ground when James admitted what it would cost.

"If you think I'm laying out two thousand pounds to save her life when she'll never be able to jump again, you've got to be joking."

Goldie's owner was obviously not one of life's great benefactors.

"We'll pay for it!" said Sarah.

Ross's eyebrows flew up into his fringe and I knew what he was thinking. The Hollywell funds were at an all-time low since we'd bought more land and ten ponies from a bankrupt trekking centre. I doubted we'd have enough to cover it.

"And we'll buy Goldie for the price you paid for her. On the condition that she retires to Hollywell Stables."

For the first time Tom Drummond actually looked nervous.

"Victor!" Suddenly a woman pushed through a gap between the ambulance and the screens and I instantly recognized her as the woman in the multicoloured hat who'd been at the Hollywell stall.

"I'm Mrs Rawlings, Victor's wife," she said in a commanding voice. "And yes, we'll take your offer. It sounds very fair."

I think I was the only one to notice Mr Rawlings' chin quivering and Drummond's teeth gritted so hard his jaw looked like a clamp.

"Mel, we'll need four rolls of gamgee and elastoplast," James ordered. "Blake, you'll have to hold her still. Sarah, we'll need a vehicle to get us down, a four-wheel drive. Ring the Animal Health Trust and tell them we're coming! We'll be there in three hours."

Drummond stormed off in a filthy temper. Within half an hour we had Goldie bandaged and loaded into the trailer, ready for the most important journey of her life.

"I'll follow in the car," Mrs Rawlings insisted. "James says I'll need to sign forms, fill in questionnaires, that sort of thing."

"What about me?" Mr Rawlings gaped, pink and puffy in the face and completely out of his depth.

"Take care of Jessica. And you'd better tell her about Goldie."

We clambered into the blue Range Rover and pulled out of the arena with the horse ambulance hitched up behind. Most of the crowds had dis-

15

persed and two of the stewards were roping off the "bridge" with some red tape. You could still see Goldie's skid marks and the ground all cut up where she'd fallen.

"The idiots," Blake hissed. "Anybody with half a brain could see this would happen."

We drove through the collecting ring at ten miles an hour. Many of the horses were still milling around waiting for the class to recommence. Daniel Lamond was slouched by one of the jumps, chatting up two girls, and he just shrugged as he saw us go past. Was that the right attitude for a professional sportsman, to win at all costs?

Trevor was staying behind to dismantle the stall and search for Katie and Danny who still hadn't appeared. Sarah was in the front with James, and Ross and Blake were in the back with me. It was going to be a long haul.

Spectators turned and watched as James made his way on to the main thoroughfare past all the new tractors and expensive car displays. Way up above us two hot air balloons hovered in the calm blue sky and the Household Cavalry was on parade in one of the other rings. That's all we'd see of the county show for this year.

"OK," James said, as we turned on to the main road out of town. "Newmarket here we come!"

It was hours before we even saw any signs for one of the most famous racing towns in the world.

James said that when he was young he dreamed of being one of the top vets in Newmarket. I was amazed at how many racehorses we saw filing down the narrow roads, often as many as thirty in one string. James had us in hysterics when he said that most people in Newmarket were short because over the years everybody who had moved there dreamed of becoming a jockey.

We drove down more leafy lanes overhung with rich red copper beech trees and squirrels running from one side of the road to the other. More racehorses passed us round the next corner and Ross swore he'd just spotted Henry Cecil riding along on a pretty grey arab.

"Look, there it is." Sarah pointed ahead and we all fell quiet as the famous Animal Health Trust came into sight. Blake, Ross and I crossed our fingers for good luck as the Range Rover swished up the sand-covered drive and we followed the arrows straight round the back for the special Clinical Unit.

It was just how I expected, with wide open spaces and immaculate brick-built stables painted in Labrador yellow and Buckingham green. Horses were popping their heads over high doors and Goldie neighed from inside the trailer, rocking it slightly on its axle.

Blake insisted that a bright bay stallion in the nearest box was a runner in this year's Derby, and when I popped my head over the door I saw a huge creamy white pot on its leg plastered well up over the knee.

Two veterinary nurses scrunched across the drive from a nearby office, followed by a man in a white coat consulting a clipboard.

"It's a clean break. But it's difficult to predict her chances – I'd say fifty-fifty."

Goldie had been led into an empty stable and one of the nurses was making her comfortable. The surgeon who was going to perform the operation was jotting down notes. "She's a very brave horse, I'll say that for her."

Mrs Rawlings was in the main office giving details of Goldie's past history.

"We'll operate tomorrow morning so expect to hear from us sometime after lunch – one way or the other."

I'd only known Goldie for a few hours but already it felt as if we were leaving one of the family.

"She's in the best of hands." Ross tried to make me feel better as we both stood stroking her neck. James was busy talking to the surgeon about X-rays and Sarah had gone off to find Mrs Rawlings.

"We're going to have to go soon." Blake leaned over the door, passing on James's message.

"But we might never see her again." The words slipped out before I realized it. We all knew that the operation was going to be incredibly difficult; if it had been her pastern or one of the small bones in . . .

"There's nothing more we can do." Ross put his arm round my shoulder, reading my thoughts. "She's been given a chance, that's the main thing."

I patted the little white star on her forehead and kissed her muzzle. "Good luck sweetheart, be brave."

We left the smell of clean woodshavings and disinfectant behind and stepped out into the drive where a thin mist of drizzle had started to fall.

Mrs Rawlings was already in her Mercedes saying goodbye to Sarah. "You've got my address and phone number. I'll expect to hear from you."

The engine purred into life and the electric window was closing as Blake shot across to her side and whipped open the car door.

"You still haven't told us how she made such a miraculous recovery." His fingers were clutching the paintwork, the knuckles showing white.

Mrs Rawlings opened and shut her mouth, completely taken aback. "I don't know what you're talking about."

"Last week at the Windsor show, I saw Goldie. She couldn't walk."

"I've already told you," she spat out, clearly

annoyed. "You obviously saw another horse. Goldie was fine. Now would you please let go of my car door?"

"She's lying." Blake was adamant. His dark eyes blazed with contempt as the Mercedes became a dot and then completely disappeared. "She's hiding something. And I for one intend to find out what."

The journey back seemed even longer and twice as tiring. We stopped at a transport café and had hamburgers which tasted like cardboard and weak coffee. We were starving and as stiff as boards by the time we'd offloaded the Range Rover and trailer and crawled up the Hollywell drive in our own car.

"Home at last." James slammed the door and Big Boris stuck his head out over his stable door, trailing a forest of hay and looking totally content.

The yard was deserted, but a tantalizing waft of fish and chips drifted from the kitchen and we dived for the back door as if we'd spent three months at the North Pole.

"So you finally made it," said Trevor, drowning a double helping of chips in tomato ketchup. Katie was feeding a battered sausage to Jigsaw, our golden Labrador. Up on the kitchen units, Oscar and Matilda, our two cats, were picking at some morsels of fish on a saucer with all the daintiness of a duke and duchess.

"Yours is in the oven." Trevor slapped Ross's wrist as he tried to grab a handful of chips. "And I've left the plates warming."

"We'll make a housewife of you yet." Sarah reached for the oven cloths and yelped when her fingers went right through the material.

"Jigsaw had hold of them earlier," Trevor said by way of explanation. "And where's the vinegar?"

We told them all about Goldie and Newmarket and the Animal Health Trust, until Katie was steaming with jealousy and complaining that we should have tried to find her and Danny.

"Serves you right for skiving off the stall," I said, sticking my tongue out.

James immediately started drawing diagrams of Goldie's leg on a sheet of kitchen roll, and Danny screwed up his face when James said they used metal staples instead of stitches and Goldie would need about a hundred. I wiped the slobber from Jigsaw's mouth (he was drooling over the remains of Oscar's fish), and Blake asked to see the address for Mrs Rawlings.

"So what did you two get up to?" Sarah looked pointedly at Katie and Danny while fishing in her handbag and pulling out a compact and a clothes peg.

Danny started stuttering and Katie pretended to get hiccups to change the subject and asked Trevor to put some keys down her back.

"I'm not getting involved!" Trevor put his empty plate in the sink, and as luck would have it the phone rang and he bolted for the hallway determined to make an escape.

"Katie?" Sarah cocked an eyebrow at my nine-year-old sister and within seconds her elfin face went bright pink.

"It wasn't our fault," she squeaked, suddenly really anxious. "You'd have done exactly the same."

"What on earth . . . ?"

I don't know whether it was the sudden silence or just pure coincidence but the most deafening screeching-bleating noise had struck up from behind the washroom door.

"It sounds like a baby crying," Ross ventured. Oscar shot through the cat flap and Jigsaw flew under the table.

"*Katie Foster!*"

Sarah flung open the door to reveal two beady, wickedly mischievous eyes glaring at her from the top of the laundry basket.

"I knew it," she shrieked. "I just knew it"

A black and white baby goat with funny, sticking-up ears and a pale pink nose barged through her legs and skidded across the kitchen tiles, ramming his tiny head into Ross's left knee. Sarah reappeared from the washroom as pale as paper, holding up her best silk skirt ripped into long thin shreds. James and Blake made a grab for the wriggly little neck just as it disappeared into Jigsaw's bowl of tinned dog food.

"His name's Spikey." Danny rubbed at the nobbly black and white head now held firmly in James's iron grip. "Nobody wanted him. Apparently he's a bit of a handful."

I was just about to declare this the understatement of the century when Trevor marched back in looking shocked, completely ignoring the eighteen-inch dynamo who was now busy chewing at James's hair.

"That was the Animal Health Trust on the phone," he said. "There was something Mrs Rawlings didn't tell us . . ."

"Let me guess." Blake took the words right out of his mouth. "They've just taken a urine sample and Goldie's been pumped full of Phenylbutazone. In other words," and he paused for dramatic effect, "she's been drugged up to the eyeballs!"

Chapter Three

"How did you know?" We all sat in a dazed state taking in the new turn in events.

Sarah scooted back from the conservatory where she'd put Spikey, and James went to ring the surgeon.

"Calculated guesswork." Blake passed round mugs of tea. "I knew right down to the pits of my boots that it was Goldie I saw last week. She couldn't have recovered that fast – it had to be drugs."

Phenylbutazone is a fine white powder commonly known as Bute, which acts as a pain-killer. It is often given to old retired horses with joint problems or horses in a lot of pain from illness. It is also illegally given to competition horses to keep them in the show-ring.

"But that's terrible!" Katie's bottom jaw had dropped open. "How do they get away with it?"

Blake explained that unlike racing, where winners are automatically tested for drugs, in show-jumping, especially at county level, it is quite easy to dope a horse and get away with it. He even knew one yard where they fed a horse sixty aspirins a day to keep it sound.

"It's unbelievable," said Ross, sweeping a hand through his black hair.

"These horses cost a fortune to keep on the circuit," Blake continued. "If Bute can keep them going, then to the owners it's worth it."

"Well, I think it stinks," I said, dropping four sugar lumps into my tea and stirring frantically.

"Yes, but Mel, what's better? A horse well looked after and able to continue enjoying his work, or being put down?"

"Nature tells us when it's time to retire," I snapped. "If a horse needs Bute then fair enough, but it should be rested, not slave-driven round endless courses of jumps."

"Hear, hear." Ross raised his mug. "Whatever happened to my shrinking violet of a sister?"

"The operation's going ahead." James came back into the kitchen. "The Bute won't have any effect. At the moment she's resting and everything seems OK. It was Mrs Rawlings who tipped them off."

"So she knew all the time." Blake's face hardened.

"What I want to know," said Katie as she fetched a chocolate cake from the fridge, "is how they get hold of the bute in the first place."

*

"Mel, don't let her wind you up, she's not worth it." Trevor poked his head over Queenie's stable door. I was grooming her so ferociously hairs were flying out in all directions.

"Ouch," I howled as the metal scraper grated against my bare leg. That was all I needed, another red mark to add to the jungle of thistle scratches. Soon I'd be able to do a dot-to-dot on my thighs.

"Mel, will you stop being so hard on yourself? You're playing straight into her hands."

I knew Trevor was right but somehow it didn't make me feel any better. The cause of my aggravation was a fifteen-year-old girl called Nicki Harris with raven-black hair and dazzling good looks, who at this precise moment I'd have liked to pack off on a one-way ticket to planet Mars.

"Maybe she's not that bad." Trevor grinned and I promptly lobbed the dandy brush at him.

From the moment Nicki had come to work at Hollywell Stables she'd made it quite clear that she was only interested in Blake and his show-jumpers. We'd advertised for ages for voluntary help over the summer holidays but as soon as people found out there was no riding they lost interest. Most of our horses and ponies were old, lame or not suitable for riding. What they needed most was love and attention and proper care, and as the sanctuary grew bigger and bigger we were becoming less equipped to provide this.

Nicki had seemed the obvious answer. She was bright and enthusiastic and had worked at the local riding school. Ross was immediately bowled over. Trevor hated her from the very beginning.

What had driven me mad this morning was that she'd made some heartless remark about Goldie being yet another useless old nag and suggested the best place for Spikey was the freezer. At this moment Goldie was fighting for her life on an operating table and all she cared about was dragging Blake down to the local shop for choc-ices.

"It's not fair, Trevor. What on earth does Blake see in her?"

It was a typically hot sticky August day and I didn't know how we were going to get through the next two hours until we heard about Goldie.

Sarah had gone off to the bank and James was working. All the horses were out in the fields, and Trevor was planning to draw straws as to who was going to start the creosoting. We'd painted all the stables but the new post and rail fencing looked as parched as paper. It was important we kept the sanctuary looking as smart as possible to impress the constant stream of visitors.

I was just about to rush into the house and answer the phone when Katie shot round the corner in a state of hysteria clutching a lead rope. "It's Spikey," she screeched. "He's gone!"

The original plan was to put Spikey in the

orchard with Snowy, our old donkey, but Snowy had gone berserk and Spikey had ended up being moved into the garden. That was a disaster too; within ten minutes he'd dug up all the bedding plants and leapt in the fish-pond.

James said he was a British Alpine and would probably have been put down because nobody wanted billy-goats, especially ones with misshapen ears and a personality problem like Spikey.

"He's on the muck heap," Danny yelled as a flurry of dirty straw spewed out like a muck spreader.

"Right, that does it," I yelled. "Spikey, I've had enough." Trevor went to answer the phone which was still ringing away and I ran across to the muck heap and leapt on top, still in my shorts and flip-flops.

What I didn't expect was the little monster to butt me on the back of my legs, sending me sprawling head first into a pile of fresh manure. "Spikey, I hate you, do you hear? You need roasting for this. I'll never forgive you."

Chaffy bits of straw stuck to my bottom lip and I was vaguely aware of a haze of midges zooming in round my head ready to go in for the kill. Spikey's beady eyes almost looked apologetic as he stared down and then he quickly decided it was some kind of game and leapt on top of me.

"Way to go, Mel."

I'd have recognized that silly tinkling laugh in Timbuctoo and would rather have died than look up into Nicki's laughing, taunting face with her perfectly glossed lips and mascara-coated eyelashes. Even worse, my own brother and Blake were cracking up too.

"Go on, have a good laugh, why don't you?" I screeched, dust-blackened and stinking like a pig farm. "I think it's absolutely hilarious." I stormed off to the house in a serious huff and swearing I'd never see the funny side of anything again.

Trevor gave me a double-take in the hallway and then charged up the stairs, grabbing hold of my arm. "That was Tom Drummond on the phone," he hissed. "He wanted to speak to Sarah."

"Did he leave a number? Did he say what it was about?"

"Give me a break, Mel, he just sees me as the dork with the purple hair."

"Maybe he's genuinely concerned about Goldie," Katie said later, as we sat in the yard, trying to catch the sun.

"And pigs might fly," Ross tutted. "He'd already got Goldie packed off to the abattoir before she'd even been X-rayed."

"Bribery," said Danny. "It's the only thing left. He wants to bribe Sarah."

"Well I don't like it." Blake threw down a copy of *Horse And Hound* which was plastered with news about Daniel Lamond. "I wouldn't trust that toad as far as I could throw him."

"Don't you think you're over-reacting?" Nicki stretched out her long legs and batted her eyelashes in Blake's direction. "I mean, it could be about anything, not just Goldie."

I inhaled sharply and tried to resist scratching at the mountain of midge bites on my neck.

"What other reason could there be?" I said. "He's hardly one of our avid supporters."

Spikey strained on his lunge rein, which was attached to the outside tap. We'd given him a wash but he still smelt awful. I'd doused myself in Sarah's expensive French perfume and now felt on the verge of fainting as it cloyed my nostrils.

It was a quarter to twelve. An hour and a quarter to go.

"What if she doesn't survive the anaesthetic?" I whimpered.

"The trouble with you, Mel, is you worry too much." Nicki pulled down the straps on her vest top to expose perfectly formed sloping shoulders. "Now if it was me . . ."

"Anyone for lemonade?" Ross opened a couple of cans, desperate to diffuse the situation.

Blake said he'd still got a Coke, and Katie gave me that knowing sister-to-sister look.

"Anyone for sun lotion?" I volunteered, practically throwing the bottle at Nicki.

"Blake, could you possibly ... I can't quite reach ..."

The little cow, I thought. She's doing it on purpose.

Nicki lazily flicked a ladybird off her arm and inched closer to Blake.

"What if her heart won't take it?" I suddenly sat bolt upright in the deck-chair. "What if she's too old?"

"Mel, stop it. We'll never get through the next hour like this." Ross stood up, visibly on edge. "Let's talk about something else."

"Like what?" I shot back, unable to picture anything but Newmarket and those ultra-clean, disinfectant-filled stables.

"Sarah's fortieth birthday."

It was Saturday, August 14th. Next weekend. Sarah was a Leo, which explained that wonderful mass of red hair and dynamic presence.

"It's a secret." Katie excitedly made notes in her horsey diary. "We're planning a party."

Nicki's finely arched eyebrows rose in immediate interest.

For weeks Sarah had been obsessed with her age; examining her imaginary wrinkles, having James in hysterics when he caught her looking at herself in the sheen of a metal saucepan. "You're

31

forty, for heaven's sake, not eighty," he grinned. "Anyway, beauty is in the eye of the beholder."

"So my neck really does look like a turkey?"

She insisted she was going to spend the whole of her birthday hiding under her duvet and if we wanted to buy her anything then it had to be a fitness video or an exercise bike.

"So a party it is then," Trevor had tormented her.

But unknown to Sarah, the idea had taken root. We'd already written out the invitations and made a start on a fantastic red and white banner.

"We'll need loads of balloons and streamers," Katie said. "And crisps and peanuts by the lorry-load."

"What about a theme?" Ross said. "Fancy dress or something?"

"Oh God," Nicki snapped irritably. "When you said a party I thought you meant a real rave, not a tea party!"

"Why do you have to be such a bitch?" I suddenly flew off the handle. "What's it got to do with you anyway – who said you were even invited?"

I could feel the blood thudding in my head and my cheeks flooding with colour. Nicki just gaped, looking really embarrassed. I couldn't help it. I was furious. And realizing that everybody was staring at me I charged off to the tack room.

Minutes later, Blake stormed in. "You didn't have to be so rude. She doesn't have to be here you know; she's working her guts out for nothing."

"Oh, don't give me that rubbish," I shouted. "You don't see her when she's painting her toe-nails and cursing the older ponies. She only shows you her goody-two-shoes side. She's a flirt and a cow and you're lapping up the attention."

I was gasping from the sheer passion of my temper and I realized I'd backed myself into a corner with nowhere to go.

"Mel, I never thought you could be like this." Blake made it worse by keeping his cool and looking at me like a disapproving schoolteacher.

"Well, I'm not perfect, OK? I'm not the sensitive, shy retiring little soul you think I am. I've got feelings and I'm not sitting back and watching you pander to her whims."

"There's no talking to you when you're like this." Blake was aghast. "I don't know what you're talking about. You're obviously seeing something that's not there."

"Oh, shut up and go away," I yelled, tears prickling hot and painful behind my eyes. "Just go, Blake. I've had enough of you."

At precisely that moment Sarah's red MG sports car stormed up the drive and the telephone burst into life. It couldn't be the Animal Health

Trust – there were still forty-five minutes to go. Unless . . .

Sarah flew into the house and Blake and I just stood looking at each other with blank expressions.

"I think," Blake finally broke the silence, "we'd better go inside."

"She's made it!" Trevor burst out of the back door, unable to contain himself. "The little cracker," he bawled, "she's pulled through!"

"You're kidding!" Blake and I could hardly believe it.

"Sarah's talking to the surgeon now," Trevor grinned, suddenly turning away as his eyes started to fill up. It was really odd, a fifteen-stone tough hunk of a nineteen-year-old getting all emotional over a strange horse. "She's made it, Mel, she's gone and shown them all."

"She's not out of the woods yet." Sarah kicked off her shoes which bounced into the dog basket, and started rummaging through a pile of papers. "The bad news is she can't come home for two weeks. But the bone's been plated, it's been a success!"

"She'll need a nice blanket." Katie started planning. "And some mints, apples, carrot cake – we can post it to her."

"Why not just get the fairies to take it?" Nicki,

who'd been quiet up to now, angled a dig but only Trevor and I heard her.

"Trevor, we need your car. Quick, I'll explain on the way." Sarah ran a hand through her hair and tried to look calm.

Trevor had recently rebuilt an entire car from the junk yard, which bumbled along at forty miles an hour. But at least we could all get in it.

"Nicki, I need you to stay behind. Keep an eye on Katie and Danny. James should be back soon." Sarah reclaimed her shoes which Jigsaw had just discovered and was about to sink his teeth into.

"Where are we going?" Ross looked as surprised as the rest of us.

"To Honeycomb Grange," Sarah read from a tatty piece of paper. "To visit Mr and Mrs Victor Rawlings!"

Chapter Four

"So it's quite simple." Sarah was explaining how owners obtained supplies of Bute.

Usually in every yard there were horses who required pain-killers at some time. It was even known for a competitor to buy in a couple of dud horses.

"The vet prescribes the necessary Bute," Sarah went on. "That's all on the level and above board. But the administration is totally in the owner's hands. All they have to do is siphon off some sachets for one of the other horses. The great thing about Bute is there's no side effects."

"It's immoral," Ross said. "Somebody should try and do something."

"But most show-jumpers are on the level." Blake turned round in the front seat. "It would be like finding a needle in a haystack, and there just isn't enough money."

"You haven't told us what we're going to see the Rawlings about," I said. "He doesn't strike me as the type to make a confession."

Sarah dug around in her handbag and passed

36

over a signed cheque. "I'm also hoping Mrs Rawlings will spill the beans. That woman knows everything. She's definitely the key."

"Here, turn left here." Sarah waved frantically. We'd been on the road for about half an hour, cutting across town and heading through the suburbs into the country. This was definitely a money part of the county; every other house looked as if it was worth a fortune.

"Trevor, can't you make this old bus go any faster?" Sarah urged. "We would like to arrive before next Christmas."

"Right you are, Mrs F." And Trevor shot the car forward at an extra ten miles an hour.

We were seriously backfiring as we turned up a long drive to pull up in front of a pink mansion with roses round the porch and an immaculate garden.

"Maybe we ought to take our shoes off," Ross joked, and I quipped back that the lawn looked as if it was regularly dry-cleaned.

"Just one thing." Ross turned to Sarah as we piled out. "How did you talk the bank manager into giving us a loan?"

"Oh that was easy." Sarah brushed off the question. "I just told him I was going to win the Romantic Novelist of the Year Award."

"You did what?"

But Sarah was already marching across to the

stable yard looking every inch a force to be reckoned with.

"My wife is in bed with a migraine." Mr Rawlings was furious that we'd just turned up unexpectedly and only softened when he saw the cheque. "I'm glad the horse is all right," he muttered. "Jessica will be pleased."

"But it doesn't solve the mystery of the Bute, does it?"

We were standing in the stable yard where there were about ten loose boxes. A couple of grooms were sweeping up, trying to listen in.

"I've already told you." Mr Rawlings' words were clipped and measured. "I know nothing about it and if you've got nothing more to say I'd like you to leave."

Mr Rawlings was getting edgy. He was dressed in tennis whites and we'd just dragged him off his own personal court where he'd been playing doubles with some friends. Without his cowboy hat he looked older and fatter in the face and he was twiddling with his tennis racket as if he wanted to hit us over the head with it.

"Don't try and lay the finger of blame on me."

"So how did it get into her system?" Sarah carried on regardless. "Don't tell me a guardian angel flew down and poured it into her evening feed."

"I've nothing more to say."

"I'm informing the BSJA," Sarah said. "And we've got the surgeon's report. There was definitely a strain in the near tendon. It could have been that which caused her to fall."

"I've got nothing to hide. If somebody put some dope in the horse's feed, then I know nothing about it."

"A little bird tells me you want to get into local politics." Sarah went in for the kill. "This kind of publicity wouldn't do you any good."

"Get off my property." For the first time Mr Rawlings looked rattled. "If you don't leave this minute I'll call the police. And get that heap of junk off my driveway."

His face was set in a hard line now. We'd pushed him to the limit. Thankfully Sarah knew when to call it a day and started backing off towards the car.

"Don't ever take the liberty of calling here again." Mr Rawlings turned on his heel and marched back to his group of friends, who were sitting on the front lawn looking decidedly edgy, not to mention curious.

"Come on gang, it's time to depart," said Sarah, glancing round. "Now where's Trevor got to?"

Suddenly we heard a toilet flush from across the other side of the yard and Trevor appeared looking apologetic. "Sorry Mrs F, I was taken short."

The two grooms had disappeared and even the horses had put their heads in, keeping well out of the way. We were no longer welcome.

"Well, at least we've paid for Goldie." Blake tried to lighten the atmosphere. "And we've probably warned him off ever trying a stunt like that again."

We climbed into the car, arguing about who was going to sit in the front, and Sarah tried to wind down the back window but the handle came off in her hand!

For a fraction of a second I thought I saw Mrs Rawlings at an upstairs window gazing down at us, but then there was nothing, just a curtain half drawn across.

"This place is amazing." Ross took one last look at Honeycomb Grange as we backfired out of the drive. "Do you realize there isn't a speck of dust in sight?"

"It's not so clean any more." Trevor turned round, grinning like a Cheshire cat. "I didn't like to mention it, but we've left about three pints of engine oil on the drive."

*

"Trevor, you're a marvel." Sarah stared down at her lap, completely lost for words.

"I found them pushed down the back of some feed bins. I could hardly believe it myself."

We were chugging through yet another immaculate village with huge yew hedges, which are so poisonous to horses, when Trevor decided to drop his bombshell. He passed Sarah three empty silver foil sachets and there was no mistaking their original content – Phenylbutazone.

"But it's not enough," Blake said a few minutes later, his face etched with frustration. "Every show-jumping yard in the country has probably got these packets stashed away somewhere. It doesn't mean anything. It doesn't mean they're doping their horses."

He was absolutely right. And we all knew it.

"But at least it's a start," I said, still bristling from our earlier run-in and determined to think positive. "Goldie was drugged, that much we do know. All we've got to do now is prove who did it."

"Oh yeah Mel, and that's going to be the easiest thing in the world to do, isn't it?"

Back at Hollywell Stables all the horses who usually came in for a feed were milling round the gate looking panic-stricken, thinking they'd been forgotten. A radio was blaring out from the tack room and Spikey was creating bedlam in the coal house. The only parts of him that weren't jet black were his beady little eyes.

It soon became obvious where the problem lay. The whole of the kitchen floor was under a good inch of water and Katie and Danny were busy mopping up with every towel they could get their hands on. Nicki grabbed a cloth as soon as we walked through the door.

"My kitchen!" Sarah howled as a stray slipper floated past.

"It was an accident." Nicky put on her sweetest face. "I didn't realize . . ."

It turned out that the glass on the washing machine door had cracked because Nicki had thrown in all the dirty horse rugs without bothering to fasten the buckles down with elastic bands. Of course she swore blind I'd never told her to do this and promptly burst into tears.

"Look," said Sarah, casting an arm about aimlessly in bewilderment. "It's been a hard day for all of us. It's nobody's fault. Just one of those things."

Katie scowled and I rescued Jigsaw's food bowl which was full of water.

"I really should be getting home." Nicki pulled

back her hair in a velvet band which perfectly complemented her dark colouring. "I've missed my bus."

"I'll drive you home." Blake leapt up, and I was even more gobsmacked when Sarah gave him the keys to her sports car.

"James hasn't rung to leave a message," Nicki deliberately stirred. "I've not heard anything. He must be working too hard, getting forgetful. Next thing he'll be forgetting birthdays."

She smiled demurely and picked up her cardigan. Sarah's brow furrowed and just for a second her eyes flickered across to the calendar on the opposite wall. The 14th of August was marked in red.

"She's awful," Katie whispered later, when we were soaking up the last of the water with bed sheets. "All the time you were out she just sat around telling us what to do. She had Danny doing all her jobs."

"She's got to go," I said, grinding my teeth.

"Yes, but what can we do?" asked Katie. "When Blake and Ross think she's fantastic, we desperately need the extra help, and she's doing Sarah's typing . . ."

Trevor came up behind us with two big steaming

43

mugs of tea, and put a comforting hand on my shoulder.

"You know what they say," he said, putting on his wiser than wise voice. "Give her enough rope and she's sure to hang herself."

"Yeah, yeah, Trevor, but something tells me our little miss Nicki is just far too clever."

Ross and Blake went off to the fish and chip shop and would no doubt be gone for ages because the girl who worked there thought they were the equivalent of Tom Cruise and Keanu Reeves and always pretended the fish wasn't quite ready.

Mrs Mac, our secretary and indispensable organiser, was away on a two-week cruise with her family and we were having a serious job coping without her. The Hollywell fan mail was growing out of all proportion and we hadn't had a decent meal for days. Mrs Mac had left a freezer full of home-prepared meals coded in different coloured tubs, but Sarah had lost the sheet of paper saying what was what and at the moment the only thing thawing on the draining board was a watery Rhubarb Surprise.

James walked in later looking completely exhausted. The floor was drying quickly but there was still the odd puddle here and there and it was as slippery as ice.

"You wouldn't believe the day I've had," James groaned, burying his head in his hands. "Surgery was absolute murder."

Sarah tried not to look upset, but it was a losing battle. Her bottom lip was quivering like a jelly and I could see she desperately needed a hug and reassurance. "You could have let us know you were going to be late," she said.

James rubbed his eyes and gave her a steady stare.

Ross and Blake came in with bags of Indian take-away.

"The chip shop has closed indefinitely," Blake said. "We've probably eaten them out of every spud in the county."

"If you must know," said James, "I've been discovering some pretty thought-provoking facts."

"I knew I'd heard the name before," James explained. "I just couldn't remember where."

We were all reeling from what James had told us, the implications slowly sinking in. I dug my teeth into an onion bhaji, wondering how people could get away with it.

"Tom Drummond." Sarah said the name out loud as if weighing it up.

"I was suspicious from the beginning when he was so keen to have Goldie put down. He was almost nervous, running scared."

"I never did like him," said Trevor, borrowing Sarah's spectacles to read the report from the Royal Veterinary College.

It was dated two years ago and contained information on a formal hearing of one Tom Drummond – an MRVCS, very lucky not to have been struck off.

Apparently, James told us, the disciplinary body always published details of any such trials and posted the full report to every vet in the country.

"At the time it was a wonder Drummond got off, but in the end there just wasn't enough proof."

Tom Drummond had been accused of fraud, falsifying insurance documents and also of being at the centre of a drugs ring in Newmarket. People paid him a fortune to get what they wanted and he willingly accepted. He'd take backhanders from anybody.

James said he personally was once offered two thousand pounds to officially state a horse unfit for use and then later when it went up for sale to say the same horse was sound.

"It's outrageous," Ross said. "I never thought vets could be so dishonest."

"Very, very few," James said. "It hardly ever happens. Anyway, as soon as I remembered all this, I rang Drummond's office and spoke to his receptionist, pretended my name was Rawlings, asked if she could check my account and bingo, Drummond has been out to see Goldie three times in the last six months."

"Sounds like we've got our man." Sarah's eyes were glittering.

"But are you sure we're not just putting two and two together and getting five?" Ross said. "What if he's gone straight?"

"I've looked into that as well." James leaned forward conspiratorially. "He's just taken a massive loan out to set up a new practice. He's in debt up to his eyeballs. And there's something else . . ."

We all waited as James caught his breath and carried on almost in a whisper. "There are rumours starting to buzz around, nobody knows for sure, but I think he's started up the same racket. What I do know is that he's trying to undercut everybody's prices and he's skimping on equipment. There have even been some complaints about his emergency service. One of my neighbour's friends swears he unplugged the phone . . ."

"The man needs locking up." Sarah was ready to go to war.

"He's a crook, I'll admit that." Thinking about it made James frown.

"So," Katie said, twiddling with the tablecloth and looking pensive. "If all this is true . . . why does he want to talk to Sarah?"

Chapter Five

"He threatened me." Sarah collapsed in the armchair with no springs. "Said if I started spreading stories I wouldn't know what had hit me. He's vicious, James. In fact he scared me to death."

I'd never seen Sarah so rattled. She was positively trembling.

"I'll kill him." Trevor snorted like a bulldog. "Nobody speaks to Mrs F like that."

"It's OK, Trevor, calm down." James pushed him back into his chair. "We need to stay rational, it's no good having slanging matches."

Katie put the stethoscope on his chest and said that his blood pressure was soaring.

"That's for his heart, you fool." Ross took the plugs out of her ears.

"Really, I'm fine," said Sarah. "If he thinks he can talk to me like that and get away with it then he's wrong."

"There's nothing more we can do tonight," said James trying to take charge. "Let's look at it in a fresh light tomorrow morning. Then decide what to do."

"Yes boss," Sarah joked.

The next day dawned bright and cheerful but soon descended towards disaster.

The first thing that went wrong was Sarah's surprise exercise video arriving by parcel post and coming within seconds of Sarah opening it. I whisked it out of her hands and buried it under some papers, cackling away that it was just one of Blake's show-jumping videos, nothing to get excited about.

What I didn't realize then was that the video I thought was Sarah's birthday present was actually something else, something far more sinister. Something that was going to mean the difference between getting off scot-free and prosecution for a certain Mr Tom Drummond.

Then Nicki arrived, decked out in the tightest pair of fawn jodphurs I'd ever seen, and new black riding boots to match.

It was part of the agreement that in return for Nicki's help, Blake would give her a free lesson. As much as I hated to admit it, she was actually quite a good rider. Last week she'd cleared nearly four foot on one of Blake's other horses, Royal Storm. But Colorado was a different kettle of fish; he was quick, sharp and temperamental. Nicki had pestered Blake until she was blue in the face and he'd reluctantly agreed to let her ride him. I was the only other person who'd ever ridden Colorado.

"Keep your heels down and your hands as light as a feather." Blake checked the girth and accidentally brushed against Nicki's leg. She gathered the reins together, grinning at me from under the velvet riding hat.

"We should have cut the stirrup leathers or put itching powder down her back," Trevor grinned as Colorado clattered out of the yard.

We were supposed to be helping Katie with Angel and Holly, our mare and foal, but we couldn't drag ourselves away.

"Just five minutes won't hurt," I giggled and we sloped off like two sleuths. I was still carrying this week's copy of *In The Saddle* which had a centre spread of Blake holding Colorado and looking dark and sultry. He'd been named Show-jumping Hunk of the Year and Sarah had pinned another copy on to the fridge door with some Blu-Tack. Blake had been mortified.

"It says here that horses only sleep for seven out of twenty-four hours," I said, flicking to the quiz page and shifting my bottom on the hard ground. "So why is old Boris permanently snoring?"

Colorado went surprisingly well at first. He had his head tucked in and was tracking up behind, moving smoothly into canter.

"You've got to give it to her," Trevor said. "She does look good on a horse."

Blake had her doing twenty-metre circles and

51

lots of transitions and then popping over small fences. It was only early morning but it was already getting hot.

We were sauntering back to the stables when we heard all the commotion. Suddenly Colorado charged into the yard, stirrups flying, riderless and his reins dangerously close to his legs. Chickens went scrabbling in all directions and Spikey started screaming his head off.

"Steady boy, whoa, whoa!" Colorado eyed me warily as I reached for the rubber reins and slowly stroked his brown and white shoulder. His long mane was thrown over both sides of his neck, and sweat was starting to trickle down from underneath. "It's all right sweetheart, nobody's going to hurt you. There, there, sssh now."

Blake came sprinting up from the field, stony-white with fear, and immediately started examining Colorado.

"It's OK," I said. "He's all right, he's not hurt."

Blake wasn't satisfied until he'd felt every inch of his body and trotted him up to see if he was lame. Colorado had always meant everything to Blake and the idea of him being hurt was incomprehensible. To say that he wrapped him in cotton wool was an understatement.

Apparently Nicki had been turning into a small spread when a bot fly had zoomed round Colorado's legs and sent him wild. Instead of reassuring him, Nicki had slapped him with the whip and Colorado had bolted towards the hedge.

"You poor baby." I stroked Colorado's throbbing nose. Bot flies are wasp-like insects which come out in August and try to lay their yellow eggs on horses' legs and under their tummies. Most horses go crazy trying to run away, and many an accident has been caused by them.

"So where's Nicki now?" I asked, undoing Colorado's grakle noseband which was all soggy with green slime.

What?" Blake looked vague.

"You know, Nicki? The junior answer to Joan Collins?"

"Oh yeah, um, she's still laid out in the hedge."

"Of all the miserable, conniving, deceitful horses I've ever ridden . . ."

We literally had to lift Nicki out of a five-foot thorn hedge and neither Trevor nor I could keep our faces straight. Somehow she'd managed to get sprawled in the middle, a bit like getting stuck in a sofa with no springs.

"I hate him. How dare he chuck me off like that." She was spitting out bits of leaves and twigs and didn't look nearly so glamorous.

"Oh, stop moaning and pull yourself together." Trevor was losing his patience.

Usually, when you fall off a horse, it's the done thing to get up as soon as possible and keep a stiff upper lip. Not Nicki, she was going to milk it for all it was worth.

"You'll not get into Blake's good books talking like that," Trevor warned. "Now dust yourself down and go and get cleaned up."

"Don't you tell me what to do." Nicki flashed her amber eyes and retrieved her whip from the long grass. "You're only the groom. Everybody knows you're as thick as two short planks."

The back of my hand shot out before I even had time to think. I swiped Nicki a stinging blow right across the left cheek and stood back and watched as her eyes nearly popped out with shock. "I've been meaning to do that for a long time."

"You, you . . . I don't believe you just did that." She was spluttering and gasping like a little kid. "W-wait till I tell Blake."

"I honestly don't think he'd be interested."

"You're crazy," she snarled, holding a hand up to her reddened cheek, her springy black hair flattened down from her riding hat, mascara clogging her eyes. "You need to see a shrink."

"Sticks and stones . . ." I warned.

"If you start acting like a decent person, you might get treated like one," Trevor told her and then marched off.

"I'll get you for this," Nicki threatened. "If you think I was trying to take Blake away from you before, then wait and see what I'm capable of. You're not going to know what's hit you."

She stood, feet apart, lips drawn back in temper, eyes dancing with venom. I was thinking I'd just set off a time-bomb. Surprisingly I felt as cool as a cucumber. I even allowed myself a faint smile.

Blake opened a gate in one of the distant fields and turned out Colorado.

"Do your worst," I muttered, swivelled on my heel and stomped back to the stables.

"I think you'd better sit down for this." The local RSPCA Inspector and Police Constable stood in our kitchen looking deeply anxious. "It's got to be kept top secret. The slightest inkling could scare them off for good."

"Wow!" Ross collapsed back in a chair as the Inspector started to tell his story.

"They don't usually start until three o'clock in the morning. They block off the traffic with old gypsy wagons and vans. They always choose dual carriageways or bypasses. There's more room you see, for more runners."

I was stunned into silence. And to think that this was going on throughout the country and we didn't know anything about it.

"It's all undercover," the Constable added. "And obviously completely illegal."

"Around ten to fifteen ponies run, and the betting is massive, huge sums of money change hands. We suspect a chap nicknamed Mad Morris from Newcastle is the ringleader. We know from a tip-off that he moved here about a year ago. Inside information told us he had a superb pony called Teddy who used to win everything. Nobody knows what's happened to him."

The idea of organized trotting races in the dead of night on motorways was so preposterous I couldn't even begin to imagine it. According to the Inspector the ponies either trotted at great speed or "paced", which was an artificial gait whereby instead of moving diagonally the hindleg and fore-leg on the same side move forward together. It was completely unnatural and the only way to get a horse moving like that was to put him in hobbles, special straps.

"It's unbelievable that they manage to get away with it." We'd all heard of loads of cases of cruelty over the last year but this was something else.

"It's so dangerous," Sarah mumbled.

"We'd like you to keep your ear to the ground. If you hear of anything suspicious, anything at all . . ." The Constable shuffled his feet, clearly upset.

"Most of these ponies end up crippled," the

Inspector was more hardened to facts. "We've got a description of Teddy," he flicked through his notebook, "a bay pony about thirteen hands with a white blaze? A bit of a character by all accounts. Chances are he'll wind up in a place like this, that's if he's still alive. The last pony we rescued in a raid had fallen and broken his back—"

"Well, we won't go into that now," the Constable quickly interrupted when he saw our faces. "If you can just keep a look-out. The man we're after is called Tommy Morris."

"Will do." Sarah showed the two men to the door.

"I don't think I'll ever be able to look at a dual carriageway in the same light again," I said instinctively picking up Oscar who was staring at us wide-eyed, and giving him a cuddle.

"The sordid details of the underworld." Ross shook his head.

"Just how can people do it?"

We were all subdued for the rest of the day and Trevor kept well out of the way, with his head under Sarah's sports car fixing the exhaust. I was wracked with guilt about slapping Nicki even though Ross said she deserved it. It still didn't make it right for me to hit her. I'd never done anything like that in my entire life.

Blake spent the afternoon schooling all four of his best show-jumpers and only broke off to guzzle three cans of Coke and talk to Ross. In ten days' time he'd be back on the circuit and it was vital he picked up a certain amount of points to get into the top twenty listing. It was also vital that somehow I patched up our tiff before it was too late. There was no sign whatsoever that he fancied Nicki and I'd completely flown off the handle.

"It's not going to be easy," Ross warned. And I knew exactly what he meant. When something bothered Blake he just retreated into his shell and nobody could get through to him. Sarah said he was an enigma and I insisted it was because he was a Scorpio. Either way I was going to have to eat humble pie.

Nicki was in the tack room when I unexpectedly barged in for a scoop of horse nuts. She had her back to me and was stretching upwards to reach the leather headcollars.

"We usually stand on one of the feed buckets," I said, trying to be friendly, a feeble attempt to break the ice.

"Oh yeah." She didn't turn round.

"Listen, I'm really sorry about earlier. I didn't mean to go that far." The words were out in the open before I realized it. "I just wanted to apologize . . ." My voice tailed off.

She didn't move for what seemed ages, and then slowly turned round with a hint of a smirk.

"That's OK, Mel, I got a bit rattled myself. Let's

just forget about it, shall we?" Her shirt still had grass stains down one side and there were scratch marks on her neck from the hedge.

"Yeah, fine," I said, and stumbled towards the door as if I'd got two left feet.

"Oh Mel, there's just one thing."

I turned round completely innocent.

"I'll be leaving an hour early today, I've cleared it with Sarah. So I won't be here for evening feeds."

"That's OK, we'll manage."

"Blake's invited me out to a restaurant."

"A little bird tells me you might need a friend." Sarah came up behind me as I leaned on the paddock fence. The rough wood of the railing grazed my cheek, but if I looked up she'd see I'd been crying.

It was a beautiful warm evening with a gentle haze of dying sun and all the ponies were crowded round the gate enjoying an early nap. Queenie and Sally were standing head to tail swishing off the flies, eyes half closed, each resting a hindleg.

"It's perfect, isn't it?"

"A little heaven," Sarah agreed, rubbing at Arnie's forehead and immediately getting covered in grease and grey hairs. "It's what we've worked so hard to create."

Every night I walked Jigsaw down into the fields and every night I marvelled at how happy and healthy all our rescue cases were, even the ones who'd been grossly mistreated like little blind Sally. They'd all found a pal and their own special place at the sanctuary. They never fought with each other or got jealous. It was as if through being a victim of cruelty they'd somehow grown wise and learned to appreciate every living moment. Trevor said it was like a permanent holiday in Majorca, which always made me laugh, but they deserved it.

"Pity we couldn't bring Teddy here," I said, breaking off a splinter of wood and digging it into the top of the rail.

"Yes, but Teddy's not what's really on your mind, is he?" Sarah got straight to the truth.

"No," I gulped, staring ahead at the reddened molten sky.

"You know once I thought someone was two-timing me." Sarah gently unpicked the knots in Arnie's mane while he stood and dozed. "I never did give him the chance to explain."

"What did you do?" I asked, suddenly curious.

"Oh, the usual thing, poured a spaghetti Bolognese over his head. Threw his car keys into a lake. Turned out he was innocent. We never could patch it up after that."

"I'm not surprised," I giggled.

"Yes, but it wasn't funny at the time. It broke my heart. What I'm trying to say, Mel, is don't leap to conclusions. Don't believe everything you see in front of you. It's often not the way it is."

"Give everybody a fair trial, is that what you mean?" I looked up despite my swollen eyes.

"It will come out in the wash, I promise you . . . Well, maybe not if Nicki's loading the machine." Sarah started to laugh, and hot tears welled up in my eyes.

"How is it," I said, giving her a massive hug, "that we all ended up with a fantastic step-mum like you?"

Chapter Six

"If you can't beat 'em, join 'em." I declared open warfare in the bathroom, clutching an eye-liner pencil and squinting into the mirror.

Katie sat on the toilet seat and pulled a face. "Mel, you look awful. You could pass for a witch."

"Katie, you wouldn't know. You're too young." I picked up the lipstick and drew a heavy line.

It was going to be another hot day but that didn't deter me from picking out a cream angora top and matching it with skin-tight black leggings. If Blake wanted glamour then that's exactly what he was going to get.

"Mel, I really don't think—"

"Katie, I've told you. I know best."

Downstairs Sarah was busy singing "Happy Birthday To Me Next Saturday" as if that wasn't the most obvious hint in the world, and James was ringing round colleagues trying to find out as much about Tom Drummond as possible. Spikey had somehow sneaked into the kitchen and was using his teeth to peel the tops off the milk bottles stashed on the floor.

"At least we're getting back to some kind of normality," Sarah said, beating up some vile pancake mixture which she insisted would be cordon bleu cuisine. "Blake's outside – he wants to talk to you."

A deep knot of nerves clenched my stomach. I couldn't go through with it, it was all a big mistake.

Sarah looked at me. "Mel, what on earth have you got on your face?"

I stepped outside into the bright sunlight and was immediately confronted by a scene I least expected. Blake was revving up his huge sponsored horsebox which took at least five horses, and Ross was carrying a pile of anti-sweat rugs and bandages from the tack room.

"I've only just heard," he leapt down from the cab, shouting over the roar of the engine. "There's an Irish-bred four-year-old going for a song on the south coast. I've got to pick it up tonight."

"But Blake?"

"I'll be back in a few days. Look after Colorado."

"Blake?"

"Don't panic. Here, catch this!"

He lobbed me a stars and stripes T-shirt which

he'd brought back from America emblazoned with "Have a nice day".

"Look after it for me," he yelled and clambered back into the cab.

I spent ten seconds gathering my thoughts before he stuck his head out of the window and gawked at my face.

"And for Christ's sake, get that muck off your face – you look awful."

Trevor insisted we went into town to track down a present for Sarah. Nicki had rolled up at lunchtime in the tightest T-shirt I'd ever seen and a new hair-do which must have cost a bomb.

As soon as she found out Blake wasn't there she stalked off to the barn in a seething fury with a snide comment that the meal had been wonderful.

"Ignore her," Trevor said. "There's got to be an explanation."

Sarah entrusted Trevor with the keys to her sports car and disappeared into the greenhouse to dwell on ideas for her latest saga. She was still insisting that she'd win the Romantic Novelist of the Year Award, and Goldie's medical bills were riding on it.

"Let's hit the road," Trevor urged just as the phone rang twice and then cut off in mid-flow.

"Must be a wrong number," I shrugged and reached for the seat-belt.

I didn't give it a second thought.

Town was heaving and the nearest we came to finding a birthday present was a horse portrait which was way over our budget. We got so desperate we even considered a lamp stand or a set of carving knives. Buying a card wasn't much better. Trevor couldn't decide between three jokey ones while I was intent on a purple badge which said "Forty Today".

I was still wearing my angora top and hovering under an overhead fan trying to cool off when I spotted Tom Drummond.

He was standing by the stationery counter flicking through a batch of half-price calendars. Nobody would have thought he'd been at the centre of a Newmarket drugs scandal, but then of course he'd never been proven guilty.

"Trevor," I hissed, backing into a promotional stand and quivering like a jelly. "Get over here quick."

Tom Drummond walked out of the store with three blank tapes. He hadn't noticed us. He marched straight through the shopping parade and disappeared from sight just as we paid for a two-foot size card with a picture of a dog on the front that looked just like Jigsaw.

"We'll write all the horses' names in it," Trevor said.

And even then they'd have to be small. We'd got more animals at Hollywell than in Noah's Ark.

We ended up buying a lovely leather briefcase with compartments for everything, and shiny gold locks. It was beautiful, and a vast improvement on anything Sarah had used before.

"We'll have to sneak it in when she's not looking," I thought aloud, batting an eyelid which had stuck together with cement-like mascara.

"Blake was right, you know," Trevor said, pressing a pedestrian light button. "You really do look a sight."

We saw him before he saw us. He was at the traffic lights in a green estate car biting his nails.

"That's him!" I shrieked, pointing through our windscreen and wondering why I was so excited.

Tom Drummond indicated left and pulled out into a stream of oncoming traffic.

"Hang on," Trevor yelled, and we wheeled out between two cars, narrowly missing a bumper.

"Trevor, what on earth do you think you're doing?"

We were four cars behind the green estate as we turned down the High Street.

"We've got an hour to kill." Trevor revved the little sports car forward. "It can't do any harm."

Considering Tom Drummond had threatened Sarah with legal action if she harassed him any further I thought it could do every harm.

"He'll spot us for sure," I squeaked. "What do you think we are, a detective agency?"

The leafy suburban streets gave way to open countryside as we rattled along at fifty miles an hour, trying to keep up. We were convinced he was heading for the Treebank Stud which bred racehorses, but instead of turning down the limestone track he cruised past and shot down a narrow lane.

"I told you I had a hunch." Trevor gripped the wheel. "He's up to something, I'm sure of it."

"Trevor, I'm not sure we should be doing this,"

The green estate slowed down and crept up a gravel track towards an old run-down barn and three mobile homes.

A man came out with two Alsatians and shook hands with Drummond, looking incredibly relieved. He was built like a rugby player, scruffy with a grisly beard and unkempt hair.

"Not exactly Buckingham Palace, is it?" Trevor whispered, winding down the window.

I insisted that we were far too close, but Trevor wouldn't listen.

"Look, what's he doing now?"

Drummond opened up the boot and lifted out a box of something or other and the three blank tapes. There was no sign of any horses on the property.

"Maybe he's come to treat one of the Alsatians?" I said, but then had doubts when they both charged off after a stick.

Drummond and the guy with the grisly beard disappeared into the nearest mobile home and slammed the door behind them.

"Now's our chance." Trevor pulled out the car keys and clicked open the tiny door. "Are you coming or what?"

We sneaked down the side of one of the buildings, which resembled an old-fashioned piggery. Sweat poured down my back like a waterfall, and my chest rose and fell in barely controlled panic. We could hear voices coming from the caravan and then a television being switched on.

We didn't find any horses. What we did find made us both catch our breath in alarm.

We slowly pushed open a half-closed door and peered into a large junk room with just a stream of light coming from a boarded-up window. It was dim and murky with a high ceiling and a cold concrete floor.

There in the corner was a green tarpaulin carelessly pulled over a lightweight structure which had flimsy bicycle-like wheels and a low-slung seat. Sprawled across one of the shafts was an equally flimsy harness, complete with reins and breast-plate. The reason it was so light was that it was made out of black PVC plastic.

I'd never seen anything like it.

"It's a sulky," Trevor breathed, running his hand along the thin shaft. "And the racing harness to go with it."

In America sulkies are used for professional trotting races on proper tracks where thorough-breds can reach incredible speeds, often nearly as fast as a racehorse.

"But there aren't any racetracks round here," I gasped, and then realized the implication of my own words.

Trevor stared at me.

"But I thought they used any old carts, not proper sulkies like this. It can't be, it's got to be a coincidence . . ."

Suddenly Trevor grabbed my arm and pulled me out of the door.

"Hurry," he hissed. "For God's sake, Mel. We could be in real danger!"

We skirted round the edge of the building in blind panic, my feet hardly touching the ground.

"Hey! Hey you! Come back!" The man with the beard plunged down the caravan steps, Drummond right behind him.

"Run, Mel, run!"

"I can't, I'm going to be sick." I'd never been more scared in my whole life. I could hardly move my legs. It brought back memories of when Ross and I had been in a scrap-yard running away from two thugs. "Trevor, I can't."

The sports car was exactly where we'd left it, pulled into the verge off the road, the doors still unlocked.

"Come on, quick!"

It was then that I heard Drummond's voice, loud and clear, bristling with authority. "Leave them be," he shouted, and then the most sickening part of all. "I know who they are."

"Trevor, he knows who we are. He recognized us!" We were sprinting along in the sports car not really knowing what we were doing or where we were going.

"Just imagine the scenario," Trevor said. "These horses get hammered on the roads, they need a vet, they need some kind of medical attention."

"But trotting races are illegal," I joined in. "Any vet getting involved would be struck off, unless he reported it."

"Tom Drummond's got no intention of reporting them." Trevor banged his fingers on the steering wheel in growing realization. "He's involved,

Mel, up to his eyeballs, and all he thinks about is lining his pockets."

The whole issue of the Bute was bad enough but trotting races as well . . . "We've got to do something, we've got to stop him!"

The wind whistled through my hair until I thought it was going to be ripped off. "Trevor, slow down. We'll end up in a ditch."

We turned into Hollywell with our nerves shot to pieces and one thing on our mind: telling Sarah.

"And that's the long and the short of it," Trevor finished off. "Drummond's a bigger crook than we thought he was and I'll bet my best shirt the man with him was Tommy Morris."

Sarah struggled to take it all in. Katie and Danny were trying to read tea leaves and predicted more surprises to come, all because they'd spotted the shape of a fox in Danny's cup.

Ross was trying to ring a telephone number which Nicki had left on a sheet of kitchen roll, someone called Betty or Letty on a five figure number which had been written down wrong.

"Somehow, some way, we've got to get proof." Sarah paced up and down twiddling a strand of her red hair. "We're not going to let him get away with it, not in a million years."

71

I stomped upstairs to take off the hundredweight of make-up still glued to my face, and Katie raced up after me with more tales about Nicki and how terrible the whole situation was getting.

"We've got to set a trap for her," said Katie plonking herself on the edge of the bath. "Did you know she's been wearing Blake's stars and stripes T-shirt all the time you've been out?"

I grabbed hold of a piece of cotton wool and screwed it up into a tight ball.

"Mel, you're not listening to me." Katie waved her hand in front of my eyes in a desperate attempt to get my attention. "And you're using the tooth-paste instead of the cleansing cream!"

Sarah marched back in from the hallway after we'd decided on our latest plan of action. "I've just spoken to the housekeeper. It's not good news, I'm afraid."

She'd been trying to contact Mr and Mrs Rawlings about Goldie and Tom Drummond.

"They're not there," she said, and went on to drop the bombshell. "They've left the country."

Chapter Seven

The next morning we discovered that Katie and Danny were right about having another surprise. Only it wasn't pleasant, not by any standards. It was a horrible mess.

Sarah's sports car, her engagement present from James, was heaped to the very brim with rotting pig muck. It was all down the sides, over the wheel, it was impossible to see the interior. It was like something out of a horror movie, only we couldn't switch off by remote control, it was there happening right in front of us.

"It's ruined." Sarah's voice was no more than a whisper. "That's it – the end."

Ross put his arm round her shaking shoulders but could find no words.

"I think we'd better phone the police," said Trevor, taking the initiative.

"Have they any idea, the sentimental value . . . Just what they've done . . ." Sarah broke off.

"It's all our fault," I blurted out. "If we hadn't gone snooping, hadn't got caught."

"It's nobody's fault, and when push comes to

shove, it's just a car. It could have been one of you."

"But what kind of people could do this?" Ross shook his head in disbelief, slowly walking round the little car that Trevor had lovingly restored and Sarah cherished.

"Oh no, the brief—" I suddenly remembered that we hadn't taken out the present. It was stuffed under the front seat and we'd been waiting to smuggle it into the house when Sarah wasn't looking.

"Ruined." Trevor's eyes filled up, swimming with water. "The hours I put into that car," he whispered, and wandered back to the house, embarrassed by his own emotion.

"This should tell us more." Ross lifted a sticky, smutted envelope from underneath one of the windscreen wipers. Inside was a typed message which made us all gasp.

"TAKE THIS AS A WARNING. WE KNOW YOU'VE GOT THE VIDEO. IF YOU EVEN THINK OF INFORMING THE COPS IT WON'T BE JUST YOUR CAR WHICH GETS WRECKED."

Video? What video? What on earth were they talking about?

Sarah read and re-read the message with trembling hands. "I don't understand, what video?"

Trevor called us in for strong cups of tea and admitted he couldn't make head nor tail of it either.

We all agreed that we should tell the police. We had to, we couldn't be held to ransom by a thug and a crooked vet. And as Sarah said, this was way out of our league, it was downright dangerous.

"He's getting back in touch as soon as he reaches the police station," Sarah said collapsing into a chair. "And I've left a message for James."

It was half past seven in the morning and the day was just beginning. Ross flung some bread on the grill and raided the fridge for the margarine. "We've got to eat," he said. "We've got to come out fighting."

Sarah squeezed my hand as I forced back tears of anger and guilt. "I'm so sorry," I said. "James will be devastated." It seemed a lifetime ago since we'd returned from France and James had asked Sarah to marry him. We'd all been so happy and the car as a present had been so romantic.

"It will be all right," Sarah insisted. "It will, I promise."

Jigsaw put his head on my knee, eyes downcast, unable to work out what was wrong. Ross and Trevor mechanically went through the process of making breakfast and I twiddled with my hair. Sarah tried to joke that I was developing nervous habits. The atmosphere was terrible. Ross went through the motions of chewing a dry crust. Trevor

75

drained and re-drained two huge mugs of tea. Danny, who hadn't said a word, lamely switched on the portable television in the kitchen and we listened to world news and watched a flamboyant chef making pancakes which Ross said were crêpes.

"I haven't seen her before," Katie squinted as a leotard-clad fitness expert took to the floor and started swirling her arms around to the music.

"The last thing on my mind is the battle of the bulge." Sarah bit her lip. She seemed to have lost half a stone in the last half hour.

"That's it!" Trevor leapt up, nearly knocking over the table with his bulk. "Mel, that video, the one you sent off for, it's the only answer. Where is it?"

Papers, newspapers, boxes of tissues, sun-tan lotion, everything went up in the air as we scoured the house for the parcel I had assumed was a fitness video.

"It's got to be that, it's the only answer." Trevor cleared a chair of papers in one fell swoop.

"Here!" Ross yelled. "It was under the cushion!"

It was a simple brown package, handwritten on the front to Hollywell Stables and marked Urgent. There was nothing to suggest who it was from. I'd obviously leapt to conclusions. There was nothing

76

inside, not even a note, just a blank tape with a title scribbled out in blue biro.

We dived through into the sitting-room and Ross slotted it into the VCR.

"Fingers crossed." Sarah perched on the sofa, leaning forward.

The screen fuzzed into life with a snowy picture and then cleared to reveal a little bay pony being put into a sulky.

"I bet that's Teddy!" Sarah grabbed my arm, nearly cutting off the blood supply.

"That's the man that was with Drummond!" I almost screeched. "Tommy Morris!"

The video cut to another scene, this time on a road. It was night-time, there were horses and vans everywhere. People were shouting. There was a huddle of people round one particular horse which was laid on its side, and a tall man in a flat cap was pushing through holding a syringe.

"It's too cloudy," Ross howled. "I can't see their faces."

The picture crackled out to nothing.

"Was that incriminating evidence or not?" Ross leapt up and rewound the tape.

"I think we've just seen our first trotting race." Sarah looked deeply shocked.

"Who sent us the video?" I asked. "How did they know about it? What's going on?"

The postmark on the envelope was local. But what did that tell us? Nothing.

"Ross, play the tape back quick. I want to have another look at the guy in the flat cap."

The phone rang and Sarah was there after two rings. "Yes, constable, I understand completely."

"What did he say?" I was frantic as soon as she'd replaced the receiver.

"There's been a new lead." She grabbed hold of the Yellow Pages and started flicking through it. "They're convinced Tommy Morris has a sister who he's probably living with, someone called Betty."

"Betty!" Ross stood stock-still in shock. "The telephone number, the one Nicki wrote down wrong . . ."

"I could throttle her." Sarah stared at the five-figure number on the scruffy piece of kitchen roll. "The silly empty-headed birdbrain. Well, there's only one thing for it. We'll have to keep making up a sixth number until we get the right one."

"But that's like picking the lock to the Crown Jewels." Ross looked gobsmacked.

"Have you got any better ideas?"

Sarah peeled back a page in the Yellow Pages giving a rundown of video specialists.

"If we can just get the picture clearer, enlarge it maybe, I'm convinced that guy in the flat cap is Drummond. He's the same build, same posture.

If we can prove it, then bingo, we've nabbed him."

"No wonder he's resorted to dumping pig muck in our car," I said.

"Ouch, don't remind me." Sarah pulled a face.

"But who sent us the video, that's what I want to know."

"Isn't it obvious?" Ross looked up, the phone in his hand. "Betty, of course."

It was no good looking in the phone book. The police had already done that. Betty would be listed under her married name which could be anything from Anderson to Ziegler.

"I can't remember." Nicki stood in the kitchen pouting.

It was two o'clock in the afternoon and she'd just turned up for her shift. The police had come round earlier and taken away the video. They'd also jotted down directions to the place where we'd seen the sulky, but no joy apparently. Wherever Tommy Morris was, if that was indeed him, he wasn't at the mobile homes.

"I've told you, I can't remember." Nicki put on her most whiny voice. "She just sounded ordinary. She didn't say anything."

"And I suppose it was her who gave you the wrong number?" Ross was unusually scathing.

"Don't blame me," she snapped. "I've always got a million jobs to do. It's not my fault if you don't have enough staff."

It was so important when running a sanctuary to take every phone call ultra-seriously. It was usually mysterious phone calls or letters which led to saving the life of a horse or a pony.

"Anyway, Mel was rather slow about the video," she sniped back.

"OK, OK, let's not start fighting," said Sarah looking world-weary. "There's nothing more we can do."

Ross had rung heaven knows how many different combinations of telephone numbers, all to no avail. And the trouble was, while he was using the phone, Betty wouldn't be able to get through. That's if she tried ringing again, which was doubtful.

"I think Teddy's half thoroughbred." Katie smudged a sponge round Queenie's eyes, which were swollen up from the flies. "Did you see how thin his legs were?"

Nicki and I took out Colorado and Royal Storm for a gentle hack, following Blake's instructions to the letter. That was one of the fantastic perks of having Blake's show-jumpers staying at Hollywell: we could help with the exercising and fitness work. Royal Storm swung forward with the most wonderful long athletic stride. He wasn't nervous and uptight like he used to be when Louella Sullivan owned him. Blake had done wonders with his temperament and his abused legs. At least Nicki wasn't as bad as Louella; she wasn't cruel to horses.

It was boiling hot as we clattered up the Hollywell drive side by side. I was really envious of Nicki's new cool white riding shirt and pale blue cotton jods and seriously wondered if she'd won the lottery.

Trevor and Ross were still stripped to the waist shovelling pig muck on to the muck heap and looking glum with the hopelessness of it all. We'd moved the car as far away from the stables as possible because horses tend to go berserk at the slightest whiff of pig muck. I still hadn't worked out why. Spikey had been locked in a stable after he'd gleefully rolled in the worst of it and Ross had set the hose-pipe on him full blast.

Sarah wandered out in a trance, looking gloomy and dejected.

I carefully washed down Royal Storm's back where the saddle mark was, and scratched under his elbow, which he always loved.

"No news," Sarah said, taking the bridle. "Not a dicky bird."

She carried out a tray of fruit juice and a packet of Jammy Dodgers which the horses polished off because none of us had an appetite.

"It's the waiting I can't stand," she said.

"We did the right thing." Ross was strong for all of us. "We had to tell the police."

"Think of a number," Sarah said out of the blue, picking a dead fly out of her glass. "Any number from one to nine."

"Eight." I pipped Katie to the post. It was my lucky number.

"Right, I'll have one more go." She drained her glass and went back into the house.

"She's really upset about the car," said Ross, rubbing a hand over his chin. "I don't know what to say for the best."

I put the horses in the field, checked the water trough which was turning slimy green, and wandered back to the stables. I was in such a dream I didn't notice Katie until she was tugging at my T-shirt.

"It's Danny," she whispered. "He's really upset. I don't know what to do."

We went into the office, where Danny was sitting on the floor surrounded by the donation boxes which we'd had specially designed and had sent to schools, clubs, libraries, shops and so on. They were made out of cardboard with a slot in the top for inserting loose change. It said on the back to send the amount collected by cheque or postal order to our address. A lot of local people had filled up boxes and then dropped them off by hand so they could have a look at the horses at the same time. It was a mammoth job counting the coins out and putting them in order. Before Mrs Mac had gone on holiday she had shown Danny and Katie exactly what to do and they'd had no problems. Until now.

Danny was close to tears. Coins were piled up all over the place and empty boxes were stacked in the corner. It didn't take me too long to work out what had happened.

"It's OK, Danny, nobody's going to shout at you. Just tell me, how much is missing?"

He swallowed hard and fought back a sob. I hated to see him so upset.

"Two hundred pounds."

The words knocked me for six.

"Mel, are you in there?" Ross blasted through the door before I could even draw breath. "It's Sarah," he said. "She thinks she's on to something."

"I rang the number," Sarah explained, "putting in an eight. A woman answered and I asked for Betty; it was her." Sarah ran a hand through her hair in excitement. "As soon as I told her I was from Hollywell Stables she put the phone down."

"Not exactly the kind of response we wanted." Ross looked frustrated.

"So what now, do we tell the police or what?" I asked. I felt as if my brain was thrumming from overload, and I couldn't take everything in.

"I don't know," Sarah said. "I honestly don't know."

We were just walking back into the kitchen when the phone rang. It was almost eerie the way it broke the silence, almost ghostly, as if it had been reading our thoughts.

"I'll get it." Sarah twitched; she was a nervous wreck.

"Yes, speaking." She'd got her voice under control. "Yes, yes . . ."

Trevor leaned on my shoulder to get closer.

"I see, yes . . ."

We couldn't hear a thing. We didn't even know if it was Betty.

"No, no, of course not." Sarah waved frantically for a pen and paper. "Yes, I understand, we'll be alone."

She started scribbling down an address in spidery writing, leaning with the phone tucked under her chin. "Give us half an hour," she finally said and slammed down the phone.

"Yes!" She almost jumped into Trevor's arms. "We've got it!"

"I presume that was the same woman ringing back," said Ross, trying to keep abreast.

Sarah kissed the piece of paper and quickly

pulled on her shoes. "Well come on, what are you waiting for?"

She hopped through to the kitchen, grabbed Trevor's car keys from the table and threw them straight at him. "We're on our way to find Teddy!"

Chapter Eight

"She sent the video," said Sarah, as Trevor crunched the gears forward and we shot down a narrow estate road which turned out to be a dead end.

"How on earth do you find this place?" We'd been travelling round in circles for the last half hour and all the roads looked exactly the same.

"Tommy Morris is her brother," Sarah said. "And he does own a pony called Teddy."

We turned into a road called Wimpole Street and hoped for the best.

"She's rung a few times and put the phone down, got cold feet at the last minute," Sarah explained.

"It's hardly surprising with a brother like Tommy Morris."

"So why is she deceiving him now?" I asked.

We came to a crossroads and took pot luck as to which way to turn. We were hopelessly lost in this huge estate and we were supposed to have met Betty ten minutes ago.

"Just keep going straight on." Sarah clung to the dashboard as we bounced over a ridge.

"Did she say anything about Teddy, anything at all?" I asked, dying to know about the little bay pony we'd seen in the video, and if he was all right.

"I don't know." Sarah's voice was low. "I think we've got to be prepared for the worst."

"There it is!" Ross pointed like mad at a sign saying Gordon Street and a house directly opposite with huge pottery shire horses filling the front windowsill. "Number six!"

As soon as we pulled up a woman came running out in faded pink slippers and a flowery slip-over pinny.

"I thought you weren't coming," she gasped. "I'd nearly given up hope."

She quickly led us along the garden path, saying that we hadn't got much time.

"But we've got the car," Sarah said. "Just tell us where he is."

Betty turned round with a look of surprise. "Oh no dear, we don't have to drive anywhere. Teddy's right here."

I nearly tripped over a paving stone in amazement. The garden was tidy but small, with neat little flower borders and a well-kept lawn – no place for a pony.

"He's over there." Betty pointed, her dress blowing up in the breeze. "In the garden shed."

None of us could speak. Nothing could take the shock away as Betty pulled back a small rusty bolt and pushed open the top half of a flimsy wooden stable door.

"Tom made this himself," Betty explained. "Just cut the door in two and screwed on some hinges."

The pony inside hunched back on its hindquarters and squinted, trying to focus in the sudden sunlight.

"He's not used to me opening the door at this time of day, are you baby. It's usually at least another hour."

Poor Teddy. I'd never seen anything quite like it. He was stuck in the shed, which had a loose scattering of straw and a bucket of water in the corner. The window was glass and made the shed a sun-trap, not to mention a death-trap if Teddy broke it with his nose. The wooden floor was soaked through with urine and the heat was unbearable. It was a tiny garden shed, not a stable.

"Why is he wearing rugs?" Sarah's voice cracked up before she could say any more.

It was a summer's day and Teddy was wrapped up in a blanket and quilt rug. His bright bay coat was soaked with sweat.

"Tom says he's got to lose some weight. He's in a big race this Saturday night."

I couldn't see much of Teddy's body, but for a thirteen-hand pony he looked incredibly lean and hard.

"He's fed oats, and the hay has to be the best, none of this off the verges or anything like that. He's well looked after."

"But Betty, he's in a shed." Sarah could stand it no longer. "He's got heat rash, he can hardly move."

For the first time Betty started to well up with emotion. "I know, I know. Why do you think I called you? Why do you think I sent the video?"

Her eyes were flooding with tears now. "And there's something else." She fished in the front pocket of her pinny and dragged out some silver foil sachets – Phenylbutazone. "I have to give him these twice a day. A big man drops them off in a month's supply. You see, what I haven't told you is that Teddy's crippled."

His hoofs were burning up. Ross and I gently felt down each foreleg with growing alarm. Even with the Bute the pain was still obvious.

"He's been racing most of his life." Betty pulled out a slice of white bread and started feeding it to him. "Nothing could ever beat him, none of the bigger horses. He was like lightning in that trap."

I ran my hand along Teddy's hard wiry neck and he looked at me with eyes that seemed to just accept his fate.

"He's a real little character you know, quite a star. But he's sixteen now, his legs can't take any more."

We led Teddy out on to the little patch of lawn and let him hobble around picking at the sweetest grass. I immediately started taking off his rugs and asking Betty for some water to wash him down.

"Tom will be back in an hour." Betty looked terrified. "He'll go berserk if he sees you here."

"There's no way we're going now." Ross spoke for all of us. "We're not putting him back in that shed."

Teddy was an exceptionally eye-catching pony, with a big white blaze down his face and two white socks behind. Even in pain he was really nosy and wanted to sniff at everything. His mane had been hogged, shaved off with clippers, which made him look younger. I vowed that when he was at Hollywell we'd let it grow back so it would keep the flies out of his eyes.

"I really think you ought to go," said Betty taking the lead rope from Ross. "I didn't want this, you don't know my brother's temper.

"How long has he known Drummond?" Sarah came right out with it. "Come on Betty, you know who I'm talking about, they're both in it together aren't they?"

"I . . . I . . ." Betty collapsed back on to a garden bench, her hands fluttering in her lap with nerves. "All I know is that a vet called Mr Drummond, the big man I was telling you about, treats Teddy.

He's got something planned for Saturday night, some kind of special injection."

Gradually in fits and starts the whole story came out. Teddy was entered for a big race on Saturday against two other experienced horses. Nobody expected Teddy to win. Everybody thought he was on the scrap heap. The betting would be in Morris's favour.

"They're convinced it will work," Betty said. "Apparently Drummond's done it before."

I could feel my eyebrows rising in shock and horror and I had to put my arm over Teddy's neck to try to convince myself that we weren't going to let it happen.

"But if they do that he'll be crippled for ever." My voice was a mere croak and I felt sick at the thought of it.

"Betty." Sarah knelt down. "If you want to help Teddy then you've got to tell us where the race will be held."

The next fifteen minutes were the most difficult of our lives.

"It's an impossible decision," I said choking back the tears. "We can't do it."

"Mel, we don't have a choice."

Teddy rubbed his forehead on my arm and then tried to drag me towards a clump of pansies, completely unaware that we were discussing his fate. His short little black tail swished at the flies, and a snail caught his attention under a stone.

"I really care about him." Betty was as upset as the rest of us. "He's just like a pet."

"It would only be for two days," Sarah said. "Just till the race. "We've got to catch them red-handed."

"But you're asking me to deliberately get my brother into trouble."

"Betty, these races have got to stop. Somebody could get seriously hurt," Sarah pleaded.

Ross took the frayed lead rope out of my hand and started leading Teddy back to the shed.

The pony's boxy crippled feet dug in and a flash of panic shot across his face. A dog barked in the next-door garden and I looked away with my jaw set rigid.

"Mel, I need your help."

As soon as Teddy was back in the shed the light drained from his face. He swivelled round and tried to push at the door as Ross pulled back the bolt.

I stroked the top of his head, the bristly bit where the forelock should have been, the bit that Trevor said felt like a toilet brush. Up to now Trevor had barely said a word. He was too flab-bergasted. It wasn't every day we found a crippled pony in a garden shed.

"Sarah's doing the right thing." He put a hand

on my shoulder. "For the sake of two days we can catch the ringleaders, put an end to it for good."

"And it's Teddy who's got to pay the price," I said gritting my teeth as a sob caught at the back of my throat.

"You've got to go." Betty bustled us down the path. "Tom will be back any minute, he mustn't suspect a thing."

Teddy's deep throaty neigh rang out up the garden with the obvious message not to leave him. Sarah walked faster and I closed my eyes, trying to shut out the noise.

"He always carries on like this when I leave him." Betty sounded almost embarrassed.

That was enough for me. I put my hands over my ears and ran back to the car, wondering for the millionth time how people could be so cruel to animals.

"Mel," said Ross, as he climbed into the back seat beside me.

"Sometimes . . ."

He put his arm round me. "I know," he said, kissing the top of my head. "It all gets too much."

"We made the right decision." Sarah marched up and down the kitchen floor. "Teddy will be all right, it's only another forty-eight hours."

James was in the kitchen with us, listening to

the story. We'd just finished talking to the police. "I'll ring them later," he said, "and arrange the final details."

I picked up Jigsaw's food, which had gone stale, and started shaking out more biscuits just for something to do.

"It's called nerve blocking," James started to explain. "From what you've told me it sounds as if Drummond is going to make two injections into the back of each fetlock. It's a bit like the injections dentists give, a local anaesthetic. It freezes up the feet within five minutes."

"And you mean after this, Teddy will be able to run completely normally?" Sarah was just checking out what we already suspected.

"It should last for about an hour. After that the poor lad will be in agony. And most likely crippled for life."

"But Morris and Drummond will have pocketed their winnings and won't care anyway."

"Exactly."

"And Drummond will have to be at the race to give this injection?"

"Yep. And if he gets caught he'll be struck off for life. He'll never be able to practise again."

"Not *if*, James." Sarah twiddled with the tea towel. "*When.*"

The phone rang. Ross answered it. He came back in, his eyes shining with anticipation.

"We've got the place," he grinned. "Betty was true to her word. It's the main dual carriageway out of town. By the industrial estates." He paused to get his breath. "Three o'clock Sunday morning!"

Chapter Nine

Waiting was a nightmare. Thinking of Teddy in that hot stuffy shed. Betty probably a bag of nerves. The police arranging a raid. It was all so tense. So undercover.

We didn't know whether we were coming or going. Trevor had us scrubbing out Sarah's car for hours on end until every trace of pig muck had disappeared. Katie had the bright idea of sticking air fresheners down the back of the seats until the whole interior smelt like a florist's shop. Luckily the briefcase was OK. We'd pushed it underneath the passenger seat, still in its carrier bag, so it was unmarked.

Blake rang to say he was on a stud farm in Cornwall and one of the tyres had dropped off the horsebox. The Animal Health Trust kept us posted about Goldie, who apparently was eating them out of house and home – and all the staff had signed her pot. They didn't know when we would be able to pick her up, but at least the leg was healing. And of course none of us knew how on earth we were going to pay for it.

Thoughts of Teddy ran through my head at least every ten minutes and Ross said if I carried on at this rate I'd be a nervous wreck in no time. Katie and Danny insisted on writing out name cards for the two empty stables, one for Goldie and the other for Teddy. I couldn't help thinking we were counting our chickens before they'd hatched. There was still time for everything to go wrong.

"Mel, don't be such a worry wart. It's all going to go exactly to plan." Trevor finished polishing the steering wheel with a final flourish, and stood back to admire his handiwork.

"Well, now you've finished that," I said, "there's something I want you to do for me."

Trevor stared down at the home perm mixture with a look of horror.

"And before you say anything, I'm not going to change my mind."

We went into the kitchen. Sarah was out at a business meeting for the morning and Ross was there, trying to unravel a pile of stable bandages.

"Trevor, just put the whole lot on. If you dither any more we'll be here till Christmas."

"But I've never permed hair before. I don't think you realize . . ."

Ross started pacing up and down, still in shock about Nicki.

"But I always thought she was so nice, I can't believe she'd do that."

"You don't know half." Trevor re-read the instructions on the perm box. "She's had Mel and me jumping through hoops since day one ... There's no doubt about it, she's pinched the two hundred pounds."

"Fancy hair-do's, expensive jods, it all adds up," I said. "It's all to impress Blake."

"All right Mel, calm down. And at least try and keep your head still."

"And she's the only one who's been using the office." I dabbed at my neck with the towel.

"To do Sarah's typing." Ross was finally getting the picture.

"I think," said Trevor as he leaned back against the sink unit, "it's time we set a trap for Nicki."

"It's bizarre." Sarah barged into the kitchen in her sherbet lemon suit, clutching a bottle of champagne. Even Jigsaw woke up in surprise, wondering what was going on.

"Forget the Romantic Novelist Award," she shrieked, rummaging in the cupboard for some clean glasses and giving up and grabbing some mugs.

"Sarah, you're not making any sense!" Ross took the foil off the champagne bottle while Sarah flipped open her bag and pulled out a contract.

"Television rights," she croaked, eyes brimming

up with tears. "For my first novel. It's going to be on the telly!"

We were all astounded. It was straight out of the blue.

"I know, I know, it's all happened so quickly. I must tell James!" Sarah didn't know whether she was coming or going.

The champagne cork flew into the yucca plant before I'd had a chance to gather my thoughts. Sarah poured champagne into the mugs.

"You mean like Barbara Cartland or Catherine Cookson, a mini-series?"

"Yes, no, I mean, oh crikey, I think I'm going to cry!"

Trevor said he'd prefer a bottle of beer and the champagne bubbles were going up his nose.

"Stardom here we come!" Ross took a gulp. "I wonder if they'll use anyone from Hollywood?"

"Never mind about the actors," Trevor said. "Just think about the money."

"We can pay Goldie's vet bill," I blurted out, realization and relief sinking in.

"All we've got to do now is rescue Teddy," said Ross, looking at his watch. "In approximately twenty-four hours."

"Oh my God!" I suddenly leapt up in panic. "My hair!"

*

The last hour before we set off for the dual carriageway was a nightmare. We were all on the verge of hysteria and I honestly didn't think we'd have got through it without Trevor's silly jokes and Sarah's constant briefs on exactly what each of us should do.

It was one o'clock in the morning and I was wide awake and counting the seconds. Trevor was just about to make another joke about wacky hairstyles when I beat him to it and rammed a tea-towel in his mouth. I couldn't bring myself to look in the mirror it was so bad and when Sarah said I looked as if I'd been plugged into an electric socket I could have sat down and cried.

"Don't let Drummond see Mel," Trevor joked. "She'll scare him off for good."

The police had informed us that they'd identified both Drummond and Morris from the video. All they had to do now was pick them up in the act, along with all the other people involved.

"It's time to go." James looked at his watch. "Operation Teddy," he joked, but we were all deadly serious.

The police were already in position when we arrived. James went across to find out exactly what was going on, and we huddled in the car not knowing what to expect. It was a dark night with barely any moon, but of course the dual carriageway would be lit up with the overhead lights.

"There's no sign of anybody yet," said James as he came back to the car. "Come on, it's time to get into position."

We could hear the odd car zooming past down below but all in all it was pretty quiet. The embankment was much steeper than I expected and even Ross was puffing when we got near to the top.

"OK everybody, it's paramount we stay out of sight, and not even a murmur." James fiddled with a walkie-talkie which linked him up to the nearest police car. There were patrols on the roundabout and at each end of the stretch of road we most expected to be used for the race.

"This is nerve-racking," Sarah hissed as we crouched down on the damp grass in complete blackness.

"Just keep thinking of Teddy," I whispered, easing myself down on my stomach so that I had a good view of the road below.

"When you see things like this in films, they never tell you about cramp." Trevor rubbed at his calf muscle, his face all screwed up.

"Or cold ground, or bugs," Ross said. He was on the other side of me with a pair of binoculars.

"What time is it?" I asked, feeling as if we'd already been there for hours.

"A quarter to three."

"What if Betty's got it wrong? What if they don't turn up?"

The road below was deathly quiet. The last vehicle we'd seen was a lorry and that had been ages ago. A tiny spider scurried across my hand, making me jump back in alarm.

"Mel, will you keep your head down. You don't know who's watching."

The walkie-talkie crackled and hissed and a deep voice came over the line asking if everything was OK.

"Never better," James answered. "But still no sign."

It was getting breezy and I pulled my cardigan closer. Twenty past three and still nothing had happened.

"They've been tipped off." Trevor cracked the bones in his fingers and shuffled position. "They've probably gone somewhere entirely different."

"Don't say that," I gasped. "Don't even think it."

I knew we'd never forgive ourselves if we'd left Teddy in danger. I crossed my fingers and saw Sarah do the same.

"There!" James whispered. "The headlights!"

Slowly, almost at a snail's pace, a convoy of vehicles came up the inside lane. They were led by a blue truck with a two-wheeled trailer on the back, which pulled over into the edge. There were voices, shouting and unravelling of chains. Two vehicles further down there was a flat-backed trailer with the sulky on board and there, climbing out of the driver's seat, was Tommy Morris.

"Got him," Ross whispered, clenching his fist.

The walkie-talkie crackled into life. "Operation Teddy. Bide your time."

We had to wait until the race was just about to start. My nerves were jangling and they hadn't even unloaded the horses yet. The blue truck unhitched its trailer and drove off with a car to effectively block off the road.

There were more people milling around now. They seemed to be appearing from nowhere, spectators of an illegal sport, keen to make a bob or two on the side. Heaven knows how much money was changing hands in betting.

Then we saw the first of the runners, a grey horse about fifteen hands, stamping and whirling around, a lovely lightweight thoroughbred with a dark mane and tail.

"Where's Drummond?" Ross's voice grated as he held up the binoculars.

"Never mind about Drummond," I said. "What about Teddy?"

And then we saw him. He was led out of a tiny trailer, still wearing rugs, his forelegs bandaged and his tail tied up high like a polo pony. He looked so tiny against the grey thoroughbred.

103

"Eh up, I think we've got our third contender." Trevor pointed down to the furthest vehicle where a heavier black horse thundered down a ramp, already wearing its harness. It was altogether chunkier with high knee action, probably some Welsh blood crossed with a hackney.

"The stage is set." James gripped the walkie-talkie, waiting through anxious moments for the police go-ahead.

There was still no sign of Drummond.

Teddy stood very quietly by the side of the trailer taking it all in. His white blaze flashed in the shadows and he hardly seemed interested in anything.

"Poor little lad," Trevor said. "He looks well cheesed-off."

Morris slapped him on the rump and moved across to a huge man unloading the sulky.

"It's got to start soon," James hissed. "It's gone half past three."

The other two horses were already being hitched up to their sulkies. One looked very home-made with pram wheels and red paint. A single kick and I think it would have smashed to smithereens.

Morris was starting to look nervous. He quickly put on Teddy's blinkers and breastplate and arranged the crupper. A crowd of people by the main throng of cars seemed to be arguing over the distance and where the race would start.

"That big guy's taking the bets," Trevor said. "I'm sure of it."

The walkie-talkie burst into life: "We've got to move in soon, stand by."

"That's him!" Ross had the binoculars. "The guy in the white riding mac, it's Drummond!"

Before we had a chance to breathe, police sirens were wailing from all directions.

"Operation Teddy, go, go, go." James threw down the walkie-talkie and we pelted down the embankment.

It all happened so fast. Flashing lights, loud-speakers, men being bundled into police vans. It was chaotic. Our main brief was to get to Teddy as soon as possible, but now we were down on the road we'd lost sight of him.

Sarah cracked her leg hard on one of the road barriers and Ross had to help her up. "Go on Mel, follow James."

Two men charged past me with police officers behind them.

"This way, Mel." Trevor grabbed my hand and we crossed over the two lanes and I suddenly saw Teddy.

He was standing frozen, completely immobilized with pain and fear, his blinkered bridle half hanging off.

"Teddy!" I yelled, and raced across, flinging my arms round his neck.

He was sweating and trembling and immediately buried his nose in my chest for reassurance. "It's all right darling, nobody's going to hurt you. It's all over."

Morris was led off with his arms locked behind his back and his face set in stone.

"I'll get you for this," he said, suddenly wheeling round, half breaking free, his mouth peeled back in temper. "I don't care how long it takes, you'd better watch your backs. I'll be after you."

"Join the queue," said Ross looking at him with disgust. "We'll be waiting."

"I think this is what we're looking for." Trevor came out of the shadows carrying a small syringe. "I found it lying on the tarmac."

James immediately said it was loaded with anaesthetic.

"There's no doubt about it," the police constable informed us moments later. "Drummond's gone. He's vanished."

Our main concern was Teddy and getting him back to Hollywell. We'd think about Drummond later.

Ross and I took the plastic harness off and James unrolled the bandages. "Now then tiger, let's have a look at these legs."

The carriageway was quickly being cleared and in another half an hour nobody would be able to tell what had happened. There'd been seventeen arrests and the police were pleased. "It's a nasty business," one officer said to Sarah. "And it's been going on too long."

I unravelled Teddy's tail which was held up with black tape, presumably to keep it out of the way of the harness and the sulky. I never stopped patting him all the time James did his examination. He was safe now, he'd never have to go back in a garden shed ever again.

"I'll have to X-ray him of course," James said. "But I think he's got a chipped fracture."

"He'll be all right though?" I asked, getting tense.

"He'll never be completely sound, I think it's too bad to operate. But," James said, rubbing at Teddy's white forehead, "he'll be able to hobble round Hollywell happily enough. I think he'll have a good life."

"I bet he'll be banging at his stable door in no time," I said, relief surging through me.

"I bet he pals up with Goldie," Trevor grinned. "They've got something in common."

"I wonder if he likes Jammy Dodgers?" Sarah laughed, and then turned away because she was crying at the same time.

Trevor and I agreed to go and fetch the horsebox while James wrapped Teddy's worst leg in what he called a Robert Jones bandage.

It was already nearly six o'clock in the morning and I couldn't believe we'd been at the dual carriageway for so long. The early dawn was beautiful and the russet sky promised another fantastic day. I was so happy I didn't even think about being up all night. Trevor started singing along to the radio and looked hurt when I told him he sounded like a strangled canary.

"It's better than looking like a cat with its coat stuck on end," he laughed, looking at my hair and then immediately apologizing when my face dropped twenty feet.

"Stop at the nearest shop," I howled. "I need a paper bag!"

We were both surprised when we turned up the Hollywell drive. Blake's giant horsebox was parked in the yard and I saw a strange horse looking out over the nearest stable door.

"He must have travelled through the night," said Trevor, weighing it up. Blake often did this between shows and I knew he wanted to get back as soon as possible.

We got out, slamming the car doors, and that's

when we heard all the noise. It sounded like a real scuffle, and it was coming from Colorado's stable.

"Blimey." Trevor ran forward. "There's a fight going on."

It was the last thing we expected. Colorado was in a corner, cowering up against the wall. Blake had his back to us, his fist clenched ready to slam into someone.

"Blake, no. Leave it." Trevor yanked open the door and charged inside. It would take a tank to stop Blake. I'd never seen him so angry.

"Leave him be," said Trevor swinging Blake's shoulder round, and for the first time I saw the other man's face. He was pressed up against the manger, his face white, his nose running with blood.

Blake was like a madman. "Get off me!" He pulled away from Trevor's grip but couldn't break loose.

"Hitting him's not the answer," said Trevor as he finally got him under control.

The other man stood gasping, one hand holding his nose, fear sketched right across his face, his knees buckling in panic. It was Tom Drummond.

It was hard to believe at first. He must have come straight from the dual carriageway. There was no doubting the hatred on his face once he realized his life wasn't in danger. "You've ruined me," he growled.

"No, you've ruined yourself," said Trevor blocking the doorway. "You deserve everything that's coming to you."

Blake fished in the woodshavings and held up a syringe. He looked in cold horror, first at Colorado, panic-stricken in the corner, and then at Tom Drummond.

I suddenly understood what had been going on.

"He tried to kill him," Blake choked. "He tried to kill Colorado!"

Chapter Ten

"Barbiturates," James said later in the kitchen. "Totally lethal. Colorado would have dropped like a fly."

Tom Drummond had been taken off to the police station and Colorado was settling down, not knowing that he'd just come within inches of losing his life.

"He obviously made a bee-line for Colorado because he knew his value," James thought aloud. "He wanted to do the most damage."

Blake was slowly recovering and Oscar insisted on climbing up his shoulder and sat purring in his ear. Katie covered some toast in orange marmalade and wanted to hear the whole story again. She and Danny had been farmed out to a neighbour last night and were itching to know every detail. I swilled down some more black coffee and wondered how I was going to keep my eyes open.

Teddy was in the intensive care unit licking madly at the mineral mint block as if he'd just discovered a sweet shop. Katie insisted she was going to introduce him to Spikey, who in all honesty was more interested in watching the chickens.

"The relief is wonderful," said Sarah. She collapsed into a chair looking dreamy. "No more money worries, no more trotting races."

"Just pure bliss." Trevor rooted out some suntan lotion which had gone green round the lid. "I think we all deserve an easy day, don't you?"

Sarah was in full agreement, and Trevor insisted on carrying out the leather armchair from the sitting-room because the deckchair had been chewed up by Spikey. Sarah said she felt really self-conscious and what would people say if they saw her sitting in an armchair in the middle of the lawn?

"Just that you're eccentric," Trevor joked. "And they know that already."

"Mel, are you going to sit in the house all day or are you going to come outside and act normal?" Blake was trying to find a new bit in a box of old tack for his new horse which from the glimpse I'd had earlier was a real stunner.

I was fluttering round the house trying to tone down my hair and wondering what sarcastic remark Nicki would make when she finally arrived.

"You are a silly mare," Blake said, which always made me laugh. "You've got beautiful blonde hair, yet you insist on trying to look like a scarecrow.

And what's all this about me taking Nicki out to a restaurant? I've never heard so much rubbish in my life."

I couldn't stop grinning for the rest of the morning. Ross said I looked as if it was my birthday and told me to keep my feet on the ground or I might float away. All I knew was that Nicki wasn't just a thief but a liar as well, and I couldn't wait till Sarah sent her packing.

Unfortunately I had to wait longer than I expected. We all agreed that the best way to set a trap for somebody was to tempt them with an irresistible prize, a bit like a piece of cheese for a mouse.

We made sure Nicki had loads of typing to do, including drafts of our new newsletter, and also made sure she was left alone in the office with ready access to heaps of coins. Trevor had rigged up a camera which he'd borrowed off a mate who'd bought it second-hand. It was a real setback when we realized it was as unreliable as Sarah's cooking and a complete waste of time.

Anyway for days Nicki showed no sign of helping herself to any money. Even Danny was beginning to think he'd got it wrong and we must have been burgled instead.

"Blake, when am I having my lesson?" Nicki strutted across the yard in buttercup-coloured jods about two sizes too small. "You did promise."

Blake said he'd been gritting his teeth and smiling at her so much his jaw ached and how much longer did he have to keep it up?

"She's not going for it at all," Ross hissed later that afternoon when Nicki still hadn't put a foot out of place.

Betty arrived around four o'clock to have a look at Teddy, and there were tears in her eyes when she saw him pottering round the orchard with Snowy, trying to reach the Granny Smith apples which were just a little too high up.

"He already looks different," she said, patting his neck which Katie had coated in fly spray. "He's getting back his old spirit."

"There's nothing like a touch of Hollywell magic." Sarah fiddled with her sunglasses which Snowy thought were edible.

"Tender loving care," I added, and swiped at a midge.

Suddenly Spikey started bleating his head off in the tack room.

"What on earth?"

"What's he doing?"

"I thought it was a baby," said Betty, spinning round in a state of panic.

"He's a baby all right." Sarah shot forward. "But not the controllable kind. Spikey!"

The scene that confronted us was utter bedlam.

Nicki was diving round the feed bins in a state of horror with Spikey charging after her, trying to butt her in the knees every time she made for the door.

"Do something," she shrieked, knocking over a tin of cod-liver oil. "He's gone crazy."

Katie and Danny were there within seconds and scooped him up just as he was about to ramrod Nicki's calves.

Trevor barged in and immediately started emptying Nicki's rucksack. A lunchbox flew across the floor followed by a lipstick and a hairbrush.

"Yes!" Trevor held up the bag of coins as if it were a trophy.

"I can explain," said Nicki, a little too quickly. "It's not how it looks."

"But it's every bit how it looks, isn't it?"

The atmosphere was terrible. You could have heard a pin drop.

"I suggest you collect your things and go." Sarah's voice was deadly calm.

Nicki was quivering all over. "You're not going to call the police, are you?" She didn't look a bit sorry.

"Just thank your lucky stars I'm not ringing them right now."

Nicki scrabbled on the floor for the lipstick and the rest of her belongings.

"Ah, if you don't mind, I'll take that." Blake reached forward for his stars and stripes T-shirt which was among the pile.

Nicki hastily did up the rucksack buckles and made for the door. "I've spent all the money. I can't give it back."

"Just go." Sarah didn't even look at her.

"You're wasting your time." Nicki reached the door and threw back one last dig. "Most of these horses should be put down. It's a waste of money."

We all stared in amazement. Sarah finally broke the silence when Nicki was half-way down the drive.

"If any of you ever keep something like this from me again there'll be big trouble, OK?"

"It's marvellous." Trevor poured out more shandy as we named Hollywell a Nicki-free zone. "We've finally got rid of her. I can't believe it."

"I wish I'd known," said Blake, looking wounded. "She's been all over me like a rash and I've only put up with it because I thought you guys liked her."

"Ah, poor Blake," I clucked, seeing the funny side now that Nicki was gone forever.

"What you call a serious breakdown in communication," Ross grinned, rearranging the fancy Union Jack flag which Spikey was wearing in honour of being such a hero. Katie was already convinced he was super-intelligent.

"I saw her take the money," Trevor said, putting a handkerchief on his head to keep the sun off. "It was purely accidental that Spikey decided to attack her."

"You've heard of Superman." Katie put on a deep voice. "Well this is Super Goat!" Spikey scowled at her and trotted off to check out the chickens. Jigsaw lay on the hot concrete watching him as if he'd just landed from outer space.

"What I want to know," I said, changing the subject, "is what are we going to do about Sarah's party?"

"It's going to take for ever," I howled as I tried in vain to handle a supermarket trolley which was fast getting out of control. Blake put in another two crates of Coke which sent the wheels skew-whiff, and the front nearly careered into a display of tinned beans.

"Balloons." Blake looked absent-minded. We must have balloons."

I set off in search of party sausages and ran into one of the local gossips who was sure to report back to Sarah exactly what was going on. I could see Blake down the next aisle signing autographs for two girls clad in jodphurs and trying to pull himself away, which was a losing battle. I still couldn't get used to him being so famous, although I had to admit to a great surge of pride.

"Next time bring a baseball cap," I grinned when he came back.

"Crisps, mini pork pies, picnic eggs, peanuts, nibbles," I read out. "You go that way and I'll go this."

Blake grabbed a pile of pony magazines and the daily papers. "OK, let's hit the check-out."

We collapsed in the car feeling emotionally battered and Blake was the first to pick up *In The Saddle*.

"There it is." He pointed with the car keys at a double-page spread attacking dangerous fences in show-jumping. After Goldie had broken her leg at the bridge, Blake had made a definite stand and was campaigning for safer courses. Everybody was behind him and there was nothing like public opinion to sway those who mattered.

"I don't think we'll be seeing any more ha-has," Blake grinned, opening up another magazine.

And thank heavens, because show-jumping against the clock is dangerous enough without creating more problems.

Back home it was even more chaotic than usual because Mrs Mac had just returned from her dream cruise.

118

"We can't tell you how much we've missed you," Sarah gushed.

"All I want to know," said Mrs Mac, casting a critical eye on our waistlines, "is have you been eating properly and what's been happening?"

"Oh," Sarah nearly burst out laughing. "Have you got three hours?"

"I'd better put the kettle on."

It was murder trying to keep preparations for the party a secret from Sarah. She kept appearing at the wrong place at the wrong time and we nearly got sprung twice. James was convinced she didn't know a thing because she kept wandering about, moaning that youth was over at forty and would James want her now that the wrinkles had set in?

The morning of the party I woke up with butterflies in my stomach and my mouth dry with nerves. We gave Sarah her cards and presents and then carried on as normal.

It was a big surprise to me though when at lunch-time Blake fished out the keys for the horse-box and announced that he and Ross would be back later.

"Talk about deserting the ship," I gasped.

"Mel, you'll be fine. Oh, and here, I meant to give you this later."

He handed me an envelope with "To Mel"

written in the corner. Inside was a card with three teddies and flowers on the front and a message: "Just To Say . . ."

I flipped it open and gasped again when I read the three special words. My eyes watered like a tap but I couldn't say anything because the pizza I was eating was stuck to the roof of my mouth. Blake winked and dived out of the door just as Sarah floated in and announced I was due at the hairdressers in half an hour.

"Mel, you look fantastic." Trevor was awestruck when I changed for the party at seven o'clock and came down the stairs dressed as a princess.

James had taken Sarah out on a pretend date and was going to blindfold her and bring her back here at half past seven. Trevor was standing at the foot of the stairs in a sumo wrestler costume and Danny was losing feathers all over the place from his Indian head-dress. Mrs Mac came in with another plate of sausage rolls and cursed for the hundredth time that nobody had told her it was fancy dress.

Guests were flooding in and the barn looked sensational. It was decked out with balloons and streamers and a big Happy Birthday banner over the door. Someone dressed as a Roman soldier was getting stuck into the sausages on sticks, but Mrs Mac had been cooking for ten thousand so I reckoned we could feed them for a week.

"Where are Ross and Blake?" I hissed to Trevor as we made our grand entrance.

"I don't know." Trevor reddened. "At the moment I'm just trying to stop this costume falling round my ankles."

I looked at my watch, which said twenty past seven, and started to get seriously worried. Surely they wouldn't miss Sarah's party? Where on earth were they?

We all hushed and held on to our drinks and James led Sarah up the yard ten minutes later. She looked radiant in a black velvet dress with her hair piled up, the star of the show. "James, if you're messing about . . ."

"Happy Birthday!" Party poppers went off and "Congratulations" struck up on the stereo. Sarah blinked in the bright light and then buried her head in James's jacket.

"I never suspected," she howled. "Not for one minute."

Trevor gave her another present, which turned out to be a new battery as a joke. Sarah clipped him over the head and Katie raced up to say that Justin Taylor had just given her a kiss but he couldn't have done it right because there were no bells ringing in her head. Danny clenched his fists and marched off to sort him out, only his head-dress fell off and was trampled on by a giant strawberry.

Suddenly an engine revved outside and someone said it sounded like a jumbo jet. I could recognize those air brakes hissing anywhere. We all dashed outside and Ross and Blake jumped out of the horsebox cab dressed as forties gangsters with false moustaches and black ties. "It's all they'd got left," Blake joked, looking particularly dashing and utterly kissable.

He wolf-whistled when he saw me and then he and Ross pulled down the ramp for the greatest surprise of the party. Goldie looked out over the partition, her soft eyes happy and content.

"The surgeon rang this morning," Ross explained. "She's made such fantastic progress she could come home early."

It was a special moment as Goldie clambered down the ramp, lifting up her plastered leg ever so carefully. She was home now, with one of the best vets to look after her and a whole team of doting assistants.

"It's the best show-stopper ever," said Danny, holding on to Katie's hand.

We all went back inside after everybody had given Goldie a pat and she'd settled into her new stable. James asked everybody to fill their glasses and said he and Sarah had a special announcement:

they'd set a date for the wedding, the 20th of October!

Mrs Mac started crying and we all applauded. "We'll have to start planning now," Mrs Mac snuffled. "We can't let anything go wrong."

"But it always does," Ross grinned.

"But it works out in the end," said Katie, looking dreamy.

The music started up and James led Sarah off on to the dancefloor.

"May I have this dance, Miss Foster?" Blake said, taking my hand.

"Well, if you insist," I grinned and I waltzed off with my arms round his neck and my feet hardly touching the ground.

"Feeling happy?" Blake gazed down at me.

"Delirious," I smiled back. "And I love you too."

"Funny," he said, frowning. "I was wondering when you were going to say that."

A selected list of titles available from Macmillan and Pan Books

The prices shown below are correct at the time of going to press. However, Macmillan Publishers reserve the right to show new retail prices on covers which may differ from those previously advertised.

All Macmillan titles can be ordered at your local bookshop or are available by post from:

**Book Service by Post
PO Box 29, Douglas, Isle of Man IM99 1BQ**

Credit cards accepted. For details:
Telephone: 01624 675137
Fax: 01624 670923
E-mail: bookshop@enterprise.net

Free postage and packing in the UK.
Overseas customers: add £1 per book (paperback)
and £3 per book (hardback).